CW00840844

For Mya-Rose

May you always fly high

and

For my Robin 2019-2020
who came into my garden
and fed out of my hand
every day

Contents

1

My Big Mistake

I want to be a Ramshackle Warrior like the rest of them. But they won't let me. 'You're too small, you're not very strong, you might get hurt, we need you here.' What they don't say is the real reason. I can't see.

'I've got a present for you,' said Jax, placing something in my lap.

Whatever it is starts to move. 'It's an animal,' I said, stroking its back, probably about the same size as Suki. But this hasn't got fur, so definitely not a kitten. The animal made tiny squeaks as I rubbed its ears and under its chin. 'He's lovely, thanks Jax.'

'I found him abandoned, poor little thing. No sign of his mum so I brought him back here. I knew you'd like him.'

'Brilliant! So now I've got a little piglet!'

'Er..no, that's the problem,' said Jax 'he's not a

piglet. He's a griffin.'

'A what?'

'A griffin. He looks like a piglet but when he gets older he'll grow wings. And wait for it, he will have the body of a lion. And the head of an eagle. You wouldn't want to meet him in the dark! Oh, sorry, Willow, I forgot you can't...'

Jax is always cracking jokes and he doesn't mean to upset me. But he is also very strong, he can pick me up with one arm. He is the tallest of all the Ramshackles. I know this because if I stand beside him I can't reach his shoulder.

'It's OK. So can I keep him?'

'It will take ages for him to grow so we can keep him indoors for now.'

'I've got a spare box next to Suki. I wonder if she'll like him.' But Suki didn't like him. She took one look at her new 'friend' and hissed and spat before hobbling off. Suki's unique. She has bright orange fur, so they tell me, and only three legs. I put Griff in the kitchen and closed the door.

'She'll get used to him,' said Jax, 'You're great

with the animals, you're our special animal agent. I'll tell everyone about him at the meeting.'

'Yeah, I want to talk about that,' I said.

Just then the door swung open as the other Ramshackles came in and took their places at the table. Once all the chairs had stopped scraping on the floor, I handed out cup cakes for everyone that I had baked earlier.

'Yummy! These are delicious,' said our leader, Regal. 'As you know we are still working on Copsil dam, the water's down to a trickle. We'll have to go under water today, swim through the pipes and then move the concrete posts blocking the flow. I want everyone helping on that one. We've also got two other problems. Ayshea, do you want to say what you've heard?' Ayshea's sitting next to me and we've been good friends ever since I arrived at Ramshackle House. She looks out for me.

'Barley Meadow. Odd things going on, they say the bees are flying backwards,' said Ayshea.

'Zubb, zubb, zubb,' laughed Jax, flapping his

arms and making a draught, 'the bees are flying backwards. Buzz buzz zubb zubb. Do you get it? Backwards?'

'Yeah, we get it, not one of your best jokes,' said Joel.

'OK, listen,' said Regal, 'we need to check this out. And something else, we haven't heard anything from Birdgirl for ages. One of us needs to make contact and see if everything's all right with her.'

I've heard of Birdgirl. She's one of our top agents. She lives in the mountains somewhere. She never comes to Ramshackle house. But she teaches all our warriors to fly. I don't know what sort of bird she is.

Regal has been the leader of the Ramshackles since I first arrived, she tells everyone what to do which I suppose is what leaders should do. She's very good at organising the gang. And she's always got a plan when something goes wrong. Sometimes it can be a very small problem the Ramshackles have to put right but sometimes it can be a very serious and even a dangerous one.

I have a wonderful time here at Ramshackle House and have such lovely friends who are kind and funny. But sometimes I get fed up.

'We have to get on, so unless anyone wants to say anything else take your positions by the terminus hub.'

'I've got something to say. I want to train as a Ramshackle warrior, like the rest of you. I know I can do it.'

The room fell silent apart from the shuffling of feet under the table. No one said anything for ages.

'OK, thanks Willow for raising this again. Unfortunately we haven't got time to discuss this today, maybe we'll think about it another time,' said Regal, her chair scraping the floor as she stood up. 'Is that OK?'

'No, it's not OK!' I said, banging my fist on the table. 'Why won't you let me join?'

'But you're vital to us here, you makes us lovely cakes and look after Ramshackle House when we're out on a mission. You're the real star,' said Regal.

'And don't forget the animals you look after and the little garden at the back,' said Coral, 'we couldn't manage without you. You love that garden.'

And that's true. I do love the garden. I grow tomatoes and lettuces and lots of herbs. Coral helps me and tells me all about the colours and size of the plants that we grow. I love the smell of mint and I can tell which herb is which by smelling them. I grow lots of flowers. I love daffodils and tiny snowdrops. I also have two rose bushes, one pink and one yellow. I can picture in my mind what each flower looks like. Sometimes I make mistakes, like pulling up flowers instead of weeds. Last week I drenched Joel with the hose but he didn't mind! The garden is my calm space. I sit on the grass and make daisy chains and listen to the birds. I'm getting quite good at learning their songs and calls. My favourite is always the robin, who comes every day and feeds out of my hand.

'I know it's lovely being here but it's not very exciting. I want an adventure, I want to do what you do.'

'You have to be super fit to be a Ramshackle,' said Jax. I hear the others murmuring and agreeing with him.

'Tell you what, we could get a special badge made just for you,' said Regal, as they got up to leave. 'Coral will sort it out when we get back.' I shrugged and didn't say any more.

Coral patted me on the shoulder as she passed. She is named after the coral reef, and has orange pink hair. I heard the terminus motor starting up and the inner door slide open. Then the tapping of the codes as each Ramshackle took their place in the hub. A sudden roar and they were gone. And I am left on my own. Again.

Suki jumped on my lap. 'I'm disappointed,' I said, stroking her back, 'It's not fair, they will never agree. I'm stuck here forever making cakes and tidying up. And guess what? They are going to make me a badge. Wow! How exciting is that! Every week it's the same. I have to stay here while they have all the fun. But wait...what if...what if I did it myself!'

I put Suki back in her basket and walked over to the door. I know exactly where the hub is. I felt for the lever at the side and pulled it down. The inner door swung open. I know the secret codes off by heart and used my fingers to brush over every letter and then tap in the code AS 424. I placed the palm of my hand on the identity screen. This is it. But which hand? I can't remember. Left or right? Left or right? Which one? The machine hummed and bleeped. The inner door closed and I felt scared. 'I've changed my mind,' I said. I pushed the button on the side to abort the mission. But the door didn't open. Instead a crackling message came through the speaker. *'Unknown Ramshackle stand by. Programme Activated. Your mission is to Save Birdgirl. Stand by for blast off.'*

'No, no, that's wrong, I've made a mistake, I'm

sorry, let me out..please.' A sudden flash and I'm catapulted through the door and sent spinning into the air at like a hundred miles an hour.

2

Find Birdgirl

'Yuk. You stink. Have you been eating garlic again?'

'Sorry my lord, I like eating stuff, especially the garlic,' said Ludo, licking his lips.

'You are a revolting creature,' said Orcusa, shifting his weight from one side of this throne to the other. It wasn't a good throne, not like a royal throne made of gold and encrusted with jewels. Orcusa's throne was made of grey metal with spikes on the arms and snake heads carved on the top. 'But you have your uses. Have you taken food to our prisoner this morning like I asked you to?'

'Yes, as you asked but it didn't take none of it and it was fresh too.'

'What did you give it?'

'Well, I made my favourite, lemon turd pancakes.'

'Lemon turds?'

'Yes, my lord, but it weren't hungry, no, I don't think it likes lemons.'

'I will go and see it now.'

Orcusa slithered across the cold stone floor and entered the dungeon. Ludo scuttled behind with a stick in his hand.

'I see you are not hungry today. Are you missing your little baybbee? Poor little precious out there on its own, all lost. Well, it's your own fault, you should have looked after it properly.'

'Yeah,' sneered Ludo, poking the stick through the bars, 'you is useless mother.' The griffin made a crying sound.

'Oh, diddums, don't cry, I shouldn't worry too much about the baby,' said Orcusa, 'it probably won't survive the night out there on its own.'

'And next time, eat my lemon turd cakes,' said Ludo poking the griffin again, 'You're lucky I don't.....AARGGH!' The griffin grabbed the stick in its ferocious jaws and snapped it in half than hurled itself against the bars so hard the ground vibrated.

Ludo fell back covering his face. 'It attacked me! It attacked me, save me, my lord, it is wild, the beast is wild.'

'Get up you snivelling coward, it never even touched you. That thing can't hurt us,' said Orcusa, 'it would take a whole army to smash down the doors.'

'So why have you got this beast in prison?' said Ludo, back in the throne room.

'Because I can,' said Orcusa, 'it shows how powerful I am. That beast is a real problem in the high mountains. But I was clever. I stole the baby and so mother griffin came looking for it and walked straight into my trap. Then I just let the baby go. Stupid griffin, might be big but got no brains.'

'What happened to the baby?'

'I don't know and I don't care. This is just the start. Now I need to find Birdgirl, I'm sure she'll come looking for the griffin.'

'Birdgirl? Is she a girl or is she a bird?'

'Stop asking me stupid questions. It doesn't

matter. She controls all the birds, millions of them, horrible, tweety, feathery little things, I hate them. And Birdgirl is also something else. She's the Princess of the Sky and a Ramshackle warrior.'

'Oh no, my lord, not them, not a Ramshackle that is bad.'

'I know. I hate them too, horrible kids always sticking their noses into other people's business. They think they are so wonderful going round doing good in the world.'

'But they are powerful.'

'Yes, and that's why I shall take them down, one by one, starting with Birdgirl. Now listen Ludo, I have a little undercover job for you.'

'I'm all ears my lord, this is exciting.'

'I want you to track down Birdgirl and bring me something back.'

'Yes, I will do this,' said Ludo, dancing around and chuckling to himself, 'then we can have a big, big feast to celebrate.'

'We will but there's one thing worse than a Ramshackle.'

'What's that my lord?'

'Your lemon turd cakes.' Orcusa touched the metal arm of this throne.

'Ah! I have a message. Well, this is interesting!' He rocked back and forward, a steely grin cracking his stone face. 'Wonderful news. There's a new Ramshackle heading our way.'

'Another Ramshackle warrior, that's more trouble for us.'

'I don't think so. Some idiot by the name of Willow just climbed into their transport hub and was zonked through into the wilderness. Ramshackle Willow. What a joke!'

'But this Willow, he could be a very strong warrior, big and hard like a willow tree.'

Orcusa roared with laughter so loud the ground shook beneath Ludo's feet.

'*He* is actually a *she*, and no, she's more like a Willow weed than a willow tree. She's not even a warrior. My spies tell me she's just a girl, useless at everything. She's not even a proper Ramshackle, she's not trained. Can't fight, can't run. She's such a coward, she's even scared of her own shadow. And best news of all, she doesn't have any protection. And she's heading our way! What fun we shall have with this weepy Willow.'

'I am so lucky to have a lord as brave and powerful as you,' said Ludo. 'So tell me, what exactly are you planning next for weedy Willow and this Birdy Girl? I hope it will be horrible, horrible and very, very scary.'

'Oh, much worse than that,' grinned Orcusa.

The Ramshackle gang arrived back at Ramshackle house, having completed their underwater dive to repair the dam.

'That went very well,' said Regal, stepping through the hub, 'should hold the water in place for a while.'

'Yeah, I 'm starving,' said Ayshea, 'hope Willow's cooking up something good for lunch.'

'That's a point. Where is she? She's not in the kitchen,' said Joel.

'We have a problem,' said Jax, 'I can't close the

hub down. Everything's jammed.'

Coral came over to the hub, and pressed the key to clear and reset. Nothing happened. No hum from the motor starting up, no flashing lights. 'It won't let me reset, I can't access the codes. Wait a minute, something's happening.' There was a hiss as the loudspeaker crackled into life.

'Access not allowed. All functions will shut down immediately.'

'What? This is wrong.'

'Unidentified person entered the hub. Codes invalid.'

'I don't understand,' said Ayshea, 'we all went together. The only person left in the house was-'

'Willow,' said Jax, tapping the identity screen. 'Look. This is her hand print. She's gone. She's gone and there's no way we can get her back.'

3

In The Ring

I landed on my feet and then fell over. All around me I felt grass. A sweet smell of candy floss filled the air. I wondered whether I had landed near a sweet stall. A fairground maybe? I called out for help but no one answered. What have I done? How do I get back? I traced my fingers over a message forming in my hand. *Find Birdgirl.* Maybe she's here and she can help me get back. Then a second message *Keep walking forward.* So I did, stopping when I reached an open entrance to somewhere.

'You must report to Mr Milner, the Ringmaster,' said a voice. Ringmaster! Then I knew where I was. A circus!

I pushed my way through the empty seats and stumbled over a circle of wooden blocks that surrounded the ring. The Ringmaster was talking loudly to someone in the centre of the ring so I followed the voice until I was close up and stood shuffling my feet in the sawdust.

'Don't do that! You'll kick up the dust,' he snarled, 'we've only just put it down.'

'Sorry, I'm Willow-

'Yes, I know who you are,' he said. 'Right, you have two chances to impress me, two chances. Either you pass or you fail. And this is your arena.'

'Flo! I want you!' Mr Milner shouted, completely ignoring me. A sudden rush of air and a rope brushed my face as a body landed perfectly on both feet beside me.

'Sorry about the rope,' said a girl, 'I'm a bit clumsy today.'

'I want you to look after Willimena,' said Mr Milner.

'It's Willow,' I said.

'She's working with us for the next two days. I want her rehearsing in the ring because she's performing tonight.'

'Performing! Performing tonight? I don't think so.'

'I've told you, either do what I ask or you fail. If you want to be a Ramshackle you do as I say.'

'Don't worry', said the girl, 'It will be all right.' She sounded about my age. 'I'm Florence but everyone calls me Flo, I perform on the high wire,' she said, 'Let's go back to my caravan. Follow me.' She walked slowly and I kept close.

'Can you see anything or are you like permanently bl.. ummm..you know..'

'Its OK, you can say it. Blind. Yes, I am. Sometimes I can make out shapes and shadows. And darkness and light. Like if the sun comes out, I can feel the warmth and I think it makes things lighter but it might be just in my head.'

'We're here now, watch the step it's a bit steep.' I heard Flo open the sliding door before guiding me inside.

'Wow! this is amazing, feels like I'm in a palace,' I said, sinking into velvet cushions, embroidered with patterns. My fingers traced the shape of the embroidery.

'Made them myself,' said Florence.

'Really? Feels so beautiful. Is it an elephant?'

'It is an elephant!'

'Are you called Birdgirl?'

'Birdgirl? No.'

'I'm supposed to be looking for her. What does Mr Milner expect me to do? I'm nervous. I can't perform tonight. I'll be useless. I'm not supposed to be here.'

'Don't worry. It's already sorted, you're being a clown tonight. Mr Charley is waiting to rehearse with you.'

'Oh, a clown,' I puffed my cheeks, 'Yeah, I can do that, clown sounds good!'

Flo took me to meet Mr Charley. He sounded really nice, not bad tempered like Mr Milner. 'So you're my new partner tonight. Have you ever been a clown before?'

'No.'

'Tonight you have to entertain, you have to make them laugh. It's going to be fun and you will love it.'

I smiled but I wasn't sure.

'OK, lets get started. Right, juggling time. Here catch!' I felt something whizz past my ear. And another and another. I did manage to catch one but then dropped it.

'Sorry, I can't do this. I can't see, I'm hopeless at catching.'

'No, you're not. This is all part of the act. I shall pretend to get cross when you drop the ball. Let's go again.' So we went again and again until Mr Charley's aim was just right and I was able to catch three balls in a row and even attempt a little juggle.

'Well done you! Amazing. Now for the main part of the act. The hoops.' He placed a hoop over my head. 'Off you go, lets see you work it.' I had done this before. I could feel the vibrations as I moved my hips around. 'Right couple more,' he said, until I had six spinning around my waist at once. 'Perfect. You'll do! See you later in the ring, Willow.'

I could hear the excited chatter of children beyond

the velvet curtain that hid the performers from the ring. Flo grabbed my arm. 'You will be fine, don't worry, and the costume looks great!' She described it to me. A bright yellow trouser suit with three red pom-poms sewn on the front. It felt a bit scratchy. Flo had spent ages putting on my make up, red cheeks on a pale cream base she said. There was something quite exciting about performing in a circus show even though I was nervous. My first task! I'm on my way. I wonder what the Ramshackles would say if they could see me now.

'Where are the clowns? We want the clowns!' bellowed Mr Milner through the microphone.

'GO!' said Flo, giving me a gentle push as the curtain parted and the spotlight picked out me and Mr Charley tottering into the ring.

'Do what I do, and remember, loud and over the top!' Mr Charley leapt on one of the blocks and yelled 'Give me a big scream and a big cheer!' Then he helped me up on a block. I shouted the same words to the audience and it was lovely to hear them yell back. But then I fell off and landed face down in the sawdust which the crowd thought was part of the act.

The hoops were something else. Mr Charley handed them to me one by one. Round and round, I was really getting into my stride. I managed to get six spinning at once. Then Mr Milner announced on the microphone.

'And now the incredible Miss Willow will attempt to spin twenty hoops at once. This has never been done before. Drum roll!'

'I can only do six at once,' I said to Mr Charley, but he couldn't hear me. The audience counted as Mr Charley threw more hoops over my head. I was getting tired and the hoops stretched from my neck down to my knees. Somehow I managed to keep them all twisting in the air.

'Twenty! She's done it!' shouted Mr Milner, 'Fantabulouso! Give it up for The Amazing Miss Willow!'

The children loved it and so did I. The act finished and I twirled two hoops on both arms. I was sorry when it was over. Mr Charley and me kept bowing and bowing until Mr Milner came in the ring and told us to get off. And all the crowd went 'Aww.' It was great fun. Flo gave me a big hug and even Mr Milner said 'Well done, Willow.'

Back in the caravan, I was too excited to sleep. 'Thank you so much Flo for helping me. I had a lovely time and I can't wait to be a clown again,' I said, pulling off my scratchy costume. 'Oh, I think I've lost a bobble. I never thought I could keep spinning all those hoops. Charley is so nice, I hope I stay here for a long time because you're my new best friend, Flo.'

'Willow,' said Flo, 'I have to tell you something.'

'Flo, I've got some more ideas for the clown act. What about if-'

'Willow! Shh. Listen! you won't be doing the clown act again.'

'Why not?'

'Because you have to do the second task. A different one, a much more important one.'

'What is it?'

Flo took her time answering. 'Tomorrow you've got to perform with me on the high wire.'

4

The Second Task

'I can't! I can't! I hate heights, I'll fall and kill myself and that will be the end. No, I'm not doing it and that's it. I'm leaving, I'm leaving right now, this has been one big huge mistake.'

Florence gently pulled me back as she perched on the caravan step.

'Listen. It's not me, I don't make the rules. You can choose not to do the second task but that's it, you fail. You are the chosen one. It's your destiny.'

'I don't want to be chosen, I just want to be me.'

'This is what training is all about. You should have thought of that before you jumped in the transport hub. I will help you, I promise you can do this. We start training in the morning.'

'I can't perform up there,' I said, pointing a finger somewhere in the sky, 'I'll be terrified!' But I had no idea just how terrifying it was going to be.

'OK, so first we'll try walking on the plank,' said Flo. I stepped onto a wide, low beam about six inches off the ground and walked slowly to the end. It was easy to balance on such a wide surface, it reminded me of the gym equipment at school. After a few tries on the beam Flo substituted a tight wire suspended from two posts, about six inches off the ground. This was much harder and I stumbled and fell off several times.

'Stop,' said Flo. 'Focus. Use your arms to help your balance, arms out straight and keep it steady. And wrap your foot around the wire. One foot at a time, keep straight, don't bend your back.' It seemed to take hours just to keep my balance let alone try and walk between the two posts. But gradually I was getting better and able to get to the end without falling off. And the wire was raised higher.

'Right,' said Florence, 'now for my six foot platform, this is your turn.'

'No, I'm not ready for that, it's too high.'

'Yes, you are, it's exactly the same whether it's six inches or six feet off the ground. As long as you remember to focus at all times and keep your head up.'

'But I might fall!'

'Yeah, you might, but we've got soft mats all around, you can't hurt yourself.'

We practised all day until I was able to walk the tightrope to the end. I had a few wobbles on the way and once I looked down and tipped over, landing on the soft cushion below. I even tried using a pole which Flo told me would help increase my balance on the wire. The pole was light and easy to manage.

'You're ready! You've been brilliant, you can do this!' said Flo, 'I'll get you a costume sorted for tonight.'

'No, I need a bit more time to practise first.'

'There is no time,' said Flo, 'It's now or never.'

It was hot standing behind the curtain but my teeth were chattering as I waited with Flo to enter the arena.

'You'll be fine, stop worrying,' said Flo. 'we do exactly what we did this morning. You look great!' I was wearing a leotard, which Flo said was sky blue, covered with lots of sparkly sequins.

Mr Milner announced the act. The curtain flew back and, holding hands, we sprinted into the centre of the ring and bowed. Flo took the microphone. 'And now ladies and gentlemen, for her first time on the high wire ever, give it up for Willow!'

The music started playing and Flo moved over towards her ladder. Where's my six foot platform? I thought, staggering around the ring with my arms outstretched, trying to find the apparatus we had used in rehearsal.

I bumped into Flo holding on to the first rung of the ladder. 'Where is it?' I hissed.

'Where's what?'

'My wire, my platform.'

'There it is,' said Flo, 'Up there. Right at the top. This is the one we use for performances.'

'What! I can't go up the ladder. It feels so high, must be like fifty feet.'

'Sixty feet, actually,' said Flo, 'but look you've got a safety net, so you can't hurt yourself. But you're not going to fall. So let's go, just follow me.'

'No, this is stupid, I'm not doing it, you've tricked me, I'm out of here.'

'All right, go on then, chicken out,' snapped Flo, 'You didn't even try. This is what you wanted. If you don't do the training you'll never make it as a Ramshackle.'

Angry tears stung my eyes. I felt Flo climb the ladder. Then I was on the ladder right behind her. 'Flo wait! I'm coming.'

'I knew you would.'

The flimsy ladder swayed from side to side as I pulled myself up, counting each rung until I reached Flo standing on the platform at the top.

'That's it, you're nearly there.' I puffed my cheeks as Flo grasped my wrists and pulled me on to the platform.

'Brilliant! You've done the hard bit!'

'Don't think so,' I said, hanging on to the guide rope. There was hardly enough room for two people to stand on the platform.

'OK, I'm going first, you follow when I get to the other side,' said Flo. 'It's not far. If I was you I'd take the pole, it will help you balance, like we did in rehearsal. Remember, it's the same wire, it's just sixty feet higher.'

The wire vibrated as Flo moved forward. She told me she would dance on the rope like a ballerina, twirling a yellow parasol in her hand and waving to the crowd below. Soon she reached the other side and called out to me.

I swallowed hard and picked up the pole. This was it. Now or never. Each time I put my foot on the wire I brought it back again. Can't do this. I'm going to fall. Be brave Willow, I thought, be brave. Ramshackles never give up.

5

Terror on the Tightrope

At last I took my first step on the high wire, then a second step, then another, wrapping my feet around the wire, remembering what I had learned in rehearsal. The pole was definitely helping me balance and I didn't feel so scared.

'Come on, you're doing fantastic,' yelled Flo. There was a slight wobble at one point. 'Keep your head straight, use the pole, focus!'

The crowd below began to chart my name, 'Willow, Willow!' I moved slowly, taking my time with every step. It was a really amazing moment and I was feeling very proud of myself.

'You're almost half way!' shouted Flo. And that's when it all started to go wrong. Something was circling around my head. I thought it was the smoke machine below that some performers used in their acts. But no. It wasn't the warm, sickly smell of the smoke machine. This was something else. A mist that was ice cold, it was sticking to my eyes and freezing my lips. The sound of the crowd chanting my name began to fade.

'Flo! Flo! I'm stuck. Help me!' But Flo didn't answer. The only sound I could hear now was the sound of rushing water coming from below. An image was forming in my head. I was walking a tightrope stretched over a gigantic waterfall, a foaming, white mass of water roaring hundreds of feet below. Heavy drops of icy water flew up and stung my face. My heart was hammering against my chest like a bass drum. One slip and I would plunge straight down into the raging fall.

I knew I had to keep going, it was my only chance. I gripped the slippery pole and the tightrope started to swing from side to side. Suddenly, a grey figure appeared on the wire just in front of me. And this thing, like an evil cloud, was closing all around me. I couldn't move, I couldn't scream.

'Willow! Come on, don't stop, you're nearly there!' It was such a relief to hear Flo again. The crowd was still chanting my name, the waterfall had disappeared and so had the grey shape. Flo took the pole, grabbed my wrists and hauled me on to the platform.

'Hey, what happened out there?'

'I don't know, I guess I panicked.'

'But you did it! Come on, let's get down.'

I slid down the rope and felt the firm ground beneath my feet again. Holding hands we took our bow and as we left the ring Mr Milner stopped me.

'Well done,' he said, 'you've passed.'

Back in the caravan I changed out of the itchy, blue leotard and sipped peppermint tea.

'You were totally amazing, I'm so proud of you,' said Flo

'I didn't think I would make it.'

I told her all about the waterfall and the grey thing that nearly got me.

'I didn't see any of that,' said Flo, 'you just seemed to freeze on the wire. I was thinking of coming to help you but I figured it might make things worse. Don't you think it was a panic attack?'

I shook my head. 'It was real, Flo, so real, especially when that shape appeared. I could see it. Something or someone wanted to make me fall, I know it did.'

'Whatever. But you passed, you're on your way, Ramshackle Girl!'

'Yeah, I'm well excited! You were fantastic Flo, I couldn't have done it without you. But tomorrow I have to go back to Ramshackle house and say sorry to everyone. Regal's not going to be very pleased with me! But maybe she'll let me stay and do more training once she knows what I've done here.'

'Mmm,' Flo sighed.

'What?'

'There's no way you can go back from here, Willow. Only forward.'

'Of course there is!'

'Not only did you break the rules when you stepped into the hub but you broke the link. You can only go back once you've completed what you've started. Your mission. Save Birdgirl.'

'But I don't want to do any more tasks, I'm happy now. I've done the tightrope. I've proved I can do it.'

'Too late.'

'Well, let me stay here, work in the circus with you. I'll do anything on the high wire, you can teach me.'

'No, you don't understand. There is no circus any more. It's gone. It's time for you to move on. I'm really sorry, Willow, but there's nothing I can do.'

'But I don't know where to go. Come with me, Flo, please don't leave me on my own.'

Flo moved forward and hugged me.

'Be brave. Be strong. We may meet again, in another world, in another time. Who knows? Goodbye, Willow.'

I clung on tightly 'I'll never forget you, Flo, you're the best friend a girl could ever have.' I felt Flo slipping away, her body dissolving in my arms 'No! No, don't leave me!' But it was too late. She was gone.

I slumped down on a patch of grass. 'What am I to do now?' I said out loud. 'Please get me back, Regal. I'm sorry I broke the rules but I did the task, I did it! I don't want to be on my own..Pl-ea-se!'

No answer. Total silence. My hand started to burn. Words were forming again in the palm of my hand. Yay! they've found me, I thought, someone's coming to get me. I tapped my fingers over the letters in my hand..two words...both the same......*Danger ! Danger!*

6

Barley Meadow

I was walking towards what? No idea. But I recognised the lovely smell of lavender nearby. I thought I could hear birds singing. Ah! This might be it. Birdgirl could be here! I bumped into a tree and gave it a hug. I'll climb the tree and maybe Birdgirl is waiting for me at the top. My next test. High above me there was noise in the sky, sounded like the engine of a small aeroplane. It wasn't easy to climb this trunk. It felt strange, the trunk wasn't rough with lots of ridges for foot holds, this trunk was really smooth. But after climbing up the tightrope, this was easy.

'Oi! What do you think you're doing?'

'Who's there?' The voice was coming from inside the
tree.

'It's me, and I don't want you messing around, breaking my petals, thank you very much, so kindly get down and leave me alone.'

'Am I talking to a tree?' I said, scratching my head.

'No. I'm a daffodil. What do you want?'

'I love daffodils! Sorry, I'm looking for Birdgirl do you know where I can find her?'

'I don't know and I don't care. So leave me alone.'

The aeroplane was getting louder and louder. NNEEOWWWWWWW. Something heavy hit my shoulder, sending me tumbling down the daffodil. I landed on a grassy bank. Two seconds later the plane landed beside me. I thought somebody might be trapped inside. I touched it with one hand. But this plane was very odd. It was soft to touch. Bit like stroking a cat. What an odd aeroplane, I thought, reaching across. It didn't have wheels. It had legs, six hairy legs, pedalling in the air. And another thing..

'AHGRR! It's a wasp! A giant wasp!' I screamed.

'I'm not a wasp, I'm a bee .Can you help me get

back up, please?'

I moved away from the giant insect-very quickly!

'Must try and save the pollen,' said the bee.

'You might sting me.'

'I won't sting you. I can't. I'm a drone, drones don't sting.'

'All right, I'll try.' I pushed and I pulled and gradually the drone slid further down the sloping bank until he managed to turn himself over.

'At least I'm upright again, thank you. I'm Martin,' he said, 'Look, my pollen sack is empty and it's all over the floor.'

'That's because you are a clumsy, stupid bee,' shouted the daffodil from above. 'And that silly girl has made a rip in one of my petals. So both of you go away.'

Martin tottered a few steps and swept a few grains of powder off his leg. 'I'm in big trouble now.'

'I'm in big trouble too,' I said, 'but maybe I can collect up some of the pollen for you.'

'Too late, I've failed again,' said Martin, 'the others will call me an idiot.'

'Hey, I'm always failing and falling over. When you get your breath back why don't you try again? Maybe I can help,' I said, thinking, here I am having a conversation now with a bee and a daffodil.

'No, I'm not supposed to be flying. I'm not a worker bee, I'm a drone. I'm supposed to stay in the hive. I came out on my own this morning to gather pollen. I wanted to show everyone that I could do it, but now it's a disaster as usual.' Martin sat down on a toadstool. 'I'm really sorry for bashing into you, I didn't see you. Don't suppose you've got any pollen you could lend me?'

'No, sorry, I wasn't after pollen. And I can't see you at all,' I said, feeling my way round the toad stall, 'I was looking for something in that daffodil which I thought was a tree.'

'Oh. What are you looking for?'

'Birdgirl. Do you know her?'

'Birdgirl? Never heard of her. Why are you

looking for her? Is she a girl? Or is she a bird?

'It's a long story. Anyway, I've failed too so I better get going. Hope you'll be all right. Try again tomorrow, Martin. Bye.'

I gave him a little wave as I walked away.

'My Queen might be able to help you,' said Martin.

'Your Queen?' I turned around.

'Yes, our Queen Bee. She knows everything. She knows all about the bees and the birds.'

'Really? Is the hive nearby?' I asked, 'Maybe I could get to see the Queen. She might be expecting me. Maybe Regal has got in touch.'

'As you helped me, I'll help you. Hop up on my back, I'll take you to the hive.'

'No, you're all right. Just point me in the right direction and I'll walk,' I said. I wasn't very happy about flying on a bee's back.

'I only know the way flying,' said Martin, 'Come on, it will be fine. I promise not to crash this time!'

Martin lowered his body to the ground so I

could climb up onto his back. I thought it might feel prickly but it was quite soft and furry.

'Hold on tight. Here we go! One, two, three take off!' Seconds later we were airborne. The wings hummed and I bent low and wrapped my arms around the back of his neck. At first it all went very smoothly, as we zoomed through the flowers, the wind rushing through my hair. That was until Martin caught his wing on a thistle which sent him swaying sharply to the right. I clung on as Martin tried to steady himself. But that only made it worse. Martin was twisting and diving through the air, it was like being on a roller-coaster with no tracks and no safety harness. And I had no idea where we were going. At one point we were flying upside down. I squealed and closed my eyes, wondering whether I would be sick before we crashed to earth again.

7

Before the Queen

Somehow Martin managed to flip back up again before landing on a dusty patch of ground. I slid off his back.

'Sorry it was a bit bumpy,' said Martin.

'So where is your hive?' I said, trying to get my breath back.

'Over there next to the old tree trunk but we're not going in the main entrance, we're using a secret passageway at the back. Hopefully, the other drones might not notice I've gone. Follow me. I'll get you in, it will be all right. The Queen likes me.'

So I followed Martin, who used his front legs to remove two tufts of grass. 'There. The secret entrance. It's dark in the tunnel. You're not frightened of the dark are you Willow?

'Huh. Everything's dark to me. But I am a bit scared going inside a bee hive.'

'Once you get inside it's fine,' said Martin, 'Just follow me, it's a bit tight to start with.' So I followed Martin and slid into the tunnel. The tunnel was damp and there was a sickly, sweet smell inside. I kept close behind Martin but not too close unless I accidentally touched his tail and got stung, even though he had told me about a million times that he didn't have a sting. Gradually, the total darkness was replaced by a strange and luminous yellow light that I could just make out.

We reached a wider part of the tunnel when Martin came to an abrupt halt and I bumped into the back of him.

'Well, well, well! If it isn't Martin. Did you enjoy your little fly around? You've been missing for two hours. The Queen's well annoyed, you're in big trouble. And serve you right for disobeying orders.'

I edged round Martin. 'Who is this?' I whispered.

'I haven't been outside, Clarence, I've been here

all the time cleaning up the secret passage, see!' said Martin, brushing the side of the tunnel with his legs.

'And who is this thing?' said Clarence, waving something in my face which tickled my cheeks, 'did you find it when you were cleaning up the rubbish?'

'I am not an it, I'm a girl,' I said.

'You're one of those live beings, we don't like you, you've come to spy on us, that's what you are, a gril being spy. Stupid Martin, you'll be punished very bad because you brought a gril spy into our hive.'

'I'm not a spy and I'm not a gril. I'm a girl, and any way it wasn't Martin's fault, he had an accident with a daffodil and I helped him up and-'

I suddenly realised what I had said..

'Oh Ho,' said Clarence, 'so you have been outside. You lied Martin.'

'I wasn't out for long Clarence, honest, I was trying to find some extra pollen for us all.'

'Save your breath for the Queen.'

I backed away wondering whether I should make a run for it when I received a painful prod in my back.

'Ouch!' I cried.

'Going somewhere, are we?' said another bee, close behind me.

'You take the gril being Claude, and I'll escort this idiot.' said Clarence.

'Where are we going?' I asked.

'To the Queen's chamber where you will both be put on trial.'

I was forced to follow Martin and Clarence as the second drone pushed me along from behind. The tunnel became wider. We entered a large area which smelt of lemon and honey and reminded me of a cough medicine that I had taken once when I was poorly. It was the hum that bothered me. A low hum that was getting louder and louder until the ground shook. I thought the ceiling and the walls might cave in. I covered my ears. Martin turned and muttered something but I couldn't hear him. I now realised where the hum was coming from. Thousands of bees surrounded me, buzzing close and hissing in my face. I thought I would fall down and wouldn't be able to get up again.

'Get back!' shouted Clarence, 'the Queen is approaching.' I was pushed into the centre of the chamber with Martin. Every bee was silent. Martin whispered that the Queen would sit on her throne in the middle of the chamber and we were not to go near her because she was guarded by very fierce female bee fighters.

'And who do we have here with Martin?' she asked.

'This is Wallow, Your Majesty, she's a gril being who has come to spy on us,' said Clarence.

'I am not a spy, I'm a girl and my name is Willow!' I said, stamping my foot.

'Silence when you're speaking to the Queen!' said Clarence, giving me a sly poke in the ribs.

'We'll deal with you in a moment, Wallow. First, step forward, Martin. I am very disappointed to hear of what you have done. Defying my direct order from yesterday. I told you drones are not allowed out of the hive. And what did you do? Flew straight out of the hive this morning without telling anyone. You disobeyed the ancient rules of the hive and you disobeyed your Queen. That is treason and you will be punished.'

'I'm sorry Your Majesty, I wanted to fly. I wanted to go on the pollen flight with the others.'

'With the female bees,' said Clarence interrupting, 'Told you once, told you a thousand times, Martin, you are a male bee and not allowed to fly with the girly bees. Your job is to guard Her Majesty in the hive. Only the female worker bees leave the hive. And you disobeyed Her Majesty the Queen,'

'Yes, all right, Clarence, I've just said all that,' said the Queen, sounding impatient.

'That's not fair, why shouldn't he be allowed to fly,' I said, 'it's a silly rule, he's only trying to help.'

'How dare you interrupt!' said the Queen.

'I wanted to bring some extra pollen to help the workers, I know we are short on pollen and we not making enough honey. That's all I wanted to do,' said Martin.

'There is indeed a crisis in the hive, we are not gathering enough pollen each day. The flowers are getting less, the meadows are not as full as they once were. Every consignment of pollen and nectar is vital to the hive and to keep us alive. Some worker bees are losing their way. All my beautiful eggs will have nothing to feed on when they hatch if we carry on like this. So tell me Martin, how much pollen did you bring back today?'

'Err mm.. I had an accident, Your Majesty I was ready to collect the pollen but as I was landing I accidentally collided with a..'

'Daffodil, I know,' said the Queen, 'and you managed to tip out all the pollen from that flower. A complete waste. You ruined the whole flight. My trusted worker bees told me the daffodil is very, very angry and so am I.'

'He's very stupid, Your Majesty, he should be severely punished,' said Clarence sneering in

Martin's face. The other bees nodded and hummed.

'He didn't mean to, it was an accident,' I said, risking another poke from Clarence, 'I saw what happened.'

'It's true,' said Martin, 'I landed on my back, and I couldn't get up and Willow saved me.'

'Why would anyone want to save you? Useless, lazy piece of junk,' said Clarence.

'That's a horrible thing to say and I think you're all horrible and this is so unfair. Martin was being kind and helpful.'

'And what about you, gril being, come here to spy on us. Did the wasps tell you to do this?' asked the Queen, 'Because wasps are our worst enemies. And you Martin, you led gril being here.'

'No, he didn't. I came here because I have to find Birdgirl,' I said, 'Martin told me you might be able to help me find her, Your Majesty.'

'Did he now. I know of no birdgirl, this is a trick. You are an enemy, coming to steal our honey.' The bees moved in closer and began hissing and buzzing again.

'No, I haven't come to steal anything. I'm a Ramshackle, I don't steal. And I'm not a spy.'

The Queen rose from her throne. 'Lies, lies and more lies. I have never heard such rubbish. It is obvious you are both guilty and you will be punished.'

'Boil them alive in honey oil,' shouted Clarence. 'he's a traitor and gril being's a thief and a spy.' All the bees started cheering and moved ever nearer to Martin and me, their hummmm increasing in volume.

'ENOUGH!' said the Queen, rising from her throne.

'Please don't hurt us,' I pleaded, 'I love bees, always have done, you're such beautiful insects.'

'I am a merciful Queen. I will spare your lives. But you, Martin, will leave the colony immediately and never return. And you gril being will go with him. And go far, far away, and never darken our hive again. If you do, the next time I will show no mercy. Dismiss.'

The guards escorted us to the main entrance. We were pushed and shoved by bees on all sides until the gate rose.

'Please don't do this Clarence, this is the only life I know, give me another chance,' pleaded Martin.

'Too late. You heard what the Queen said. It's goodbye and good riddance to you!' And with that he gave Martin a quick kick up his back side and pushed him out. I followed closely behind, 'And don't ever come back.'

8

Our New Friends

Then it started to rain and rain and rain. Cold and dripping wet, we sheltered under a bush for hours, both feeling very sorry for ourselves.

'I tried my best,' said Martin, 'I just knew it wouldn't work out for me, it never does.'

'I think they were horrible to you, especially that Clarence. Yes, you tried your best.'

'No, they are right. I am a useless bee, my fault for wanting to fly and losing all the pollen in that daffodil. No one likes me. Now I've been thrown out of the nest. Total failure, as usual. I can never find the lavender, I always get it mixed up with all the other flowers and weeds. They are all the same colour, how am I to know which is which? No wonder I'm useless.'

'I think Clarence is a very nasty bee and....what did you just say about all the flowers being the same colour?'

'Well, they are. If the lavender in the field was a different colour it would be easier to find.'

'What colour do you think lavender is?'

'Grey, like the rest.'

'What about that daffodil?'

'Grey,'

'What's the colour of my hair, Martin?'

'Grey.'

'No, it's red. And lavender is not grey, it's blue. And daffodils are yellow.'

'I don't understand.'

'I do. Martin, you're colour blind, that means you don't see any colours except grey. I reckon we can fix this for you.'

'But how do you know this because you can't see either.'

'No, but other people tell me. In my mind I can see all the different colours.'

'It doesn't matter now. The Queen won't let me back in the hive, so I'm homeless,' said Martin.

'I'm a failure too. And there's no way I can get

back home or see my friends ever ever again,' I said, sniffing back the tears.

'You're not a failure, Willow. You're a very brave girl and you saved my life otherwise I would have still been lying on my back in that field, at the mercy of any animal or wasp or spider that wanted to eat me.'

'Eat you? Why would I want to do that?' said a voice from above. I heard something slither down the tree trunk and land just in front of us, quickly followed by another.

'Wasps!' hissed Martin.

'We're friends,' said the wasp. 'I'm Riley and this is Ray.'

Martin backed away into a bush, pulling me with him. I could feel his body trembling. 'Wasps have always been our enemies,' said Martin. 'Go away or I will call my friends from the hive and you'll be sorry.'

'Hmm, probably not, as you've just been thrown out of the hive and no one likes you,' said Riley.

'We heard every word,' said Ray.

'Just let us go, we won't cause you any trouble,' I said, 'It's been a bad day.'

'We're not going to hurt you, we want to help you. Don't we Ray? OK, so wasps and bees have been mortal enemies in the past but now we've got a peace plan. We can't go on fighting for ever, and we can help you and your friend get back to the hive.'

'I don't live in the hive,' I said.

'But don't you want to see Martin become a hero? And all the other bees will say how wonderful he is. And human girl, you can help us.'

'Huh. And how's that going to happen?' said Martin, still keeping his distance.

'Right, listen carefully. Up there in the tree,' said Riley, 'we've got a stack of pollen and nectar, loads of it. Enough to feed you and loads for the Queen's babies when they hatch.'

'Wasps don't collect pollen, so that's not true,' said Martin.

'I think they do, Martin,' I said.

'Open that sack and show him, Ray.' The second wasp opened a sack and dipped in his leg and took out a cup full of sweet smelling nectar. 'The very best. Try it.' Martin was frightened but so hungry and he couldn't resist the offer. He stuck out his tongue and lapped up the delicious nectar.

'Well? Excellent stuff isn't it?'

'It's lovely but I don't understand why you are being so nice to us,' said Martin.

'Listen,' said Riley, 'We will take loads of pollen sacks and nectar to the bee hive especially for the baby bees when they hatch, and you guys can help us. When all of your bee buddies see this they will let you back in again. We'll say it was your idea to save the hive. And then we'll sign a peace agreement. Bees and wasps will be friends forever and you Martin will be a hero. And in the future we can share the meadow lands and help each other, and never fight again.'

'Umm,' said Martin, hesitating, 'I suppose it might be worth a try.'

'Good, that's settled then. Me and Ray will go and get the stuff ready and we'll all go together. Just one problem though, if me and Ray turn up at the front entrance of the hive the guards will attack us straight away. We could be killed before we've had a chance to explain what we are doing. The peace plan will be ruined.'

'I never thought of that, I guess our plan is not going to work. What a shame,' said Ray. He sounded really upset.

'If only there was another way into the hive where we could deliver the nectar and pollen first, then convince your Queen that we are friends,' said Riley.

'What about the secret entrance where you took me?' I said.

'Shh! That's a secret, that's where the Queen's eggs are stored. We can't possibly do that,' said Martin.

'Well, it's not a secret now is it? But that would be perfect,' said Riley, 'we can store the pollen and nectar right next to the eggs, be a surprise. The

Queen will be ever so grateful and we can all have a big feast to celebrate. What do you say Martin? You're big chance to become one of the most famous bees in the land.'

'I don't think I should,' said Martin.

'If you don't want to do it we'll find another bee who will and you'll both end up failures again. See yer.' Riley flew back up the tree.

'No, wait,' said Martin, 'All right, I'll help you. You don't have to come,Willow.'

I chewed my lip. 'I'm not letting you go on your own.'

'We've got nothing to lose,' said Martin.

'We shall fly out late this afternoon and enter the hive when the honey bees are still busy collecting pollen. We'll have this sorted in no time!' said Riley.

I clung onto Martin's back as he led the way to the hive. Riley flew alongside him, very close. Soon we were joined by several more wasps who flew in close formation. I could hear their stings sliding in and out as a warning to any enemies.

'Don't worry about them,' shouted Riley, 'they are just extra handlers, they've all got little sacks of pollen for your bees.'

Riley stopped all the wasps as they hovered a few feet above the ground.

'Right, now you Martin, are going to get us in the secret tunnel. Some of my guards will distract the bees at the front entrance. We don't want to get mashed up when we're bringing such lovely goodies.'

Martin guided Riley and four other wasps round the grassy bank at the back of the hive. I slipped off his back as we made a bumpy landing.

'Nice one, Martin,' said Riley, 'let's get this door open. And you, my friend, will soon be the hero of the hive.'

Martin burrowed in the long grass until he found the secret hatch made of twigs and roots.

'So where exactly are these eggs?' said Riley.

9

Traitors become Heroes

'They're tucked away in a corner.'

'That's good. We can leave the pollen and be back out in no time. You go first, Martin, and then we'll follow, in case there are any guards about.'

Martin led the way followed by me. There was only one drone guarding the passage, the others had gone to the front, fearing a massive wasp attack on the main entrance.

'It's all right,' said Martin, 'we come in peace. These are nice wasps they're bringing all this pollen for the Queen's eggs, and-'

'We haven't got time for this,' snapped Riley, pushing past Martin, 'Let's find these eggs.'

'Oi!' You can't go any further!' shouted the drone. I felt Riley move in close, drawing his vicious sting.

'One more squeak out of you and you'll be a

dead bee, got it?' The drone moved back.

'Don't worry about him,' said Riley, 'we don't want some useless drone messing up our peace agreement. Get your sacks ready boys, looks like we've found the eggs. Look, there's a huge pile of them! Perfect, these will make a nice feast for the others when they join us from Motley Wood.'

'You two,' he said to Martin and me, 'start picking them eggs up and pass back to us, reckon we can manage about twenty in each bag.'

'What are you doing? Are you taking the eggs? You said you were bringing pollen for the babies when they hatched,' said Martin.

'I lied,' laughed Riley. 'You shouldn't believe everything you're told. Anyway, what do you care? They slung you out of the hive. Now get moving before I get really cross!' The other wasps buzzed around us and I could feel them draw their stings.

'All right,' said Martin, picking up an egg and handing it to Riley.

'That's more like it,' said Riley 'now the rest.

Pass it down the line boys. Soon as your sack is full, crawl out backwards to the entrance and wait for me.'

'Martin, we've been tricked, you can't do this!' I said.

Martin moved in closer and whispered 'Trust me.'

The wasps continued loading their sacks until they could take no more. Martin told me all the eggs were gone.

'We are done here. This should make sure there will be no baby bees born this year,' said Riley, 'Soon we'll control all of this hive when our battalions of wasps arrive. And you'll be extinct. Bye bye bees and girly thing, thanks for your help. Losers.'

I sank to my knees. 'What have we done? What have we done Martin? I wished I'd never started this.'

'Shhh! Come outside, I want to show you something, come on quickly.'

'What's the point? The wasps have tricked us and we were stupid enough to listen,' I said.

'Here,' said Martin, placing a heavy wooden club in my hand, 'it's for protection in case we get attacked. Now follow me, Willow, this isn't over yet.'

Riley was waiting in the entrance. I followed Martin down the secret tunnel and out through the hatch just as the wasps were regrouping. I heard them all take off, heading back to Motley Wood.

'Oh, great, the wasps are flying away with the stolen eggs, thanks to us.'

'WAIT!' said Martin. Before I could say anything else there was a loud bang, followed by another, then another, then another, like a hundred balloons popping all at once.

'What's happening? Are the wasps exploding?'

'Not the wasps, it's the eggs,' said Martin, 'brilliant isn't it?'

'No, it's horrible all those baby bees in those eggs,' I said gazing up into the sky, following the sounds of exploding eggs.

'But they're not. The babies are safe and sound in the egg fortress behind the Queen's throne.

What the wasps have stolen are decoy eggs, they're not real ones! And they're full of rubbish.'

'How do you know?' I said

'I know because that's my job. I collect all the rubbish, all the goo, all the poo, all the snot, then I make them into an egg, and when they are dry I stack them in the secret tunnel. So if anyone takes these they get a nasty shock because as soon as the decoy eggs hit the air, Bang! they explode.'

One by one the wasps, covered in slime, crashed to the ground, their wings matted together. 'They won't be able to fly again until they get rid of this goo, it will take weeks! It's a long walk back to Motley Woods,' laughed Martin, turning to face me. That's when I heard it, the sound of an angry wasp buzzing towards us at full power.

'LOOK OUT!' I screamed.

'Die stupid drone, die!' shrieked Riley. It was too late for Martin to escape. But not too late for me. I stood in front of Martin and swung the wooden club in my hand, hoping it wouldn't miss the target. I knew I would only get one chance to stop him before the sting pierced poor Martin. I felt the rush of air then Smack! I caught Riley a hefty blow just inches away from us.

'He's crashed into a pine tree,' said Martin.

I sighed and sank to my knees. 'Are you all right Martin? He didn't sting you?'

'Yeah, I'm OK, he missed. You saved my life, again!'

'Getting a bit of a habit!' I said, just as hundreds of worker bees soared from the sky and landed nearby taking Riley prisoner.

Ava, the flight Commander of the squadron, walked up to Martin. 'I think you've got some explaining to do,' she said.

We spent a long time with Queen Bee. I told her everything that had happened. She called a special meeting of all the bees in the hive and told them that she believed Martin was telling the truth.

'He wanted to come back to the hive and hoped the wasps' peace plan would work. But he didn't trust them which is why he took them to the decoy eggs once he realised what they were really trying to do.

'And in doing so, he saved us all. The hive will work for another year thanks to Martin. So Martin will return permanently to the hive and I have decided that under your guidance, Ava, he will be allowed to fly with other worker bees gathering pollen. He will need some special training to avoid accidents and to make sure that he doesn't fly backwards.' The others laughed and I suddenly thought of what Jax had said in Ramshackle House on that day before I left.

'But I am confident this brave little drone will succeed,' the Queen continued, 'And something else. Willow told me that Martin can't see the colours of the flowers in the fields. We shall arrange for him to wear special coloured goggles, so he will be able to see all the different colours.' Martin jumped up and down in excitement!

'Thank you, thank you, thank you Your Majesty!'

All the bees started chanting Martin's name and

patting him on the back, apart from Clarence.

'You can't do that,' said Clarence, 'he's just a mucker out. Who's going to clean all the dirty poo out of the hive?'

'Well, Clarence, there's now a vacancy, it's obviously a very important job so I've decided that you will take Martin's place.' For once Clarence was silent. He was furious.

'And as for you Willow, you stood in front of Martin and faced the vicious wasp leader, Riley. Such bravery! And in honour of saving Martin's life, not once but twice, you are granted the freedom of the hive. Without you and Martin, the hive would have been destroyed by the wasps. Now we have a future. You may stay here and live amongst us for as long as you wish.' I felt very sad and bit my lip before answering.

'Thank you, Your Majesty, that's very kind but I can't stay here. I must go home. But first I have to find Birdgirl. If I don't complete my mission I can never go back.'

'I wish we could help. I have heard of this

Birdgirl but she is too far away for us to find her.'

Now all the bees were chanting my name.

'I think it's time we celebrated,' said the Queen, 'bring my special honey jars, there's enough for everyone.'

'Please change your mind and stay,' said Martin, the next morning, as I prepared to leave, 'You're the best friend I've ever had.'

'I would love to stay but I can't. I'm not a bee. This is not my life. This is not my home. I must go on to try and find Birdgirl. Besides, you will have loads of friends now. And you've got flying adventures to look forward to.'

I walked towards the centre of the meadow. Martin started to cry. He gave me a special stick that the others had made to help me find my way.

'I shall never forget you, Willow, you're the bravest, loveliest being I have ever met,'

'No one has ever said that to me before.' I hugged him tightly. 'Goodbye, dear friend, I hope we meet again someday.'

10

The Land of the Wicked Way

Back in the castle basement Ludo was munching his third lemon turd tart and feeling very pleased with himself when Orcusa's voice boomed down the stairway.

'Ludo! Up here now!'

'Yes, my lord, I'm on my way.'

In his chamber, Orcusa held out his hand. 'Where is it?'

'It's here my lord.'

'Ah! I have it at last. Look at this Ludo, a thing of beauty, don't you think?' The Emerald stone. See how it shines. '

'I can see my face in it,' said Ludo.

'That's not good. But you have done well Ludo, very well. Birdy Girl's power is finished, her reign is over. But she doesn't know that yet.

And now I have the stone, I have the power.

'Will she come and try to get it back?'

'Most certainly. That's when the fun starts when she and weepy Willow reach my castle.'

'Tell me, tell me!'

'You'll have to wait and see. But for now I am also aware we have others heading our way. Enemies. More of them. Ramshackle rejects.'

'That's not good, my lord, not good. Too many. Don't like them.'

'No need to worry, Ludo. They have just crossed into the Land of the Wicked Way. But my new defence shield will stop them getting any further. The are flying straight into a trap.'

'How much longer?' asked Jax, putting his feet on the table.

'I can't do it any quicker, I'm doing my best,' answered Coral, as she worked on the control panel in the hub.

'I know. I'm sorry, it's just I can't bear to think of Willow out there, lost and on her own. I feel so helpless.'

'We're going to get her back, don't worry,' said Regal.

'Yes!' The panel lit up with a line of orange and green lights. 'We're back,' said Coral.

'Well done, Coral! So let's see if the computer can give us any help,' said Regal, pressing the speech and communication button. 'OK, Red alert. Where is Willow?'

Have no information,,unidentified intruder entered hub. Has been transported out of Ramshackle House

'Yeah, but where? We know all this. You must have some idea,' said Regal, having an argument with the computer.

Information registered shows that intruder activated the Mission objective, Saving Birdgirl. Now heading in the direction of the Land of the Wicked Way.

Coral gasped and put her hand to her mouth when she heard that. Jax broke the silence. 'What are we going to do?'

'We are going to find her, that's what we're going to do,' said Coral, already pulling on her Ramshackle jump suit. 'Come on.'

'Hang on, We can't all go,' said Regal, 'Dave and Ayshea, stay here in case Willow finds her way back again. Coral and Jax, you come with me. And you, Joel. And you, Madeleine. Prepare to activate the hub in five minutes.'

Coral had set the coordinates so they would arrive close to the border with the land of the Wicked Way. The hub could propel them no further. Regal knew the Ramshackle warriors would now have to fly into very dangerous territory.

'This is Orcusa's land,' said Regal. The others nodded.

'But he never comes here,' said Jax, 'We haven't seen or heard of him for ages. Why would he be interested in little Willow, she's no threat to him?'

'I hope you're right, Jax. I hope you're right. But why is Willow trying to save Birdgirl? Sounds really odd. That's why we need to find her and soon.'

The land in front of them was very rocky with no vegetation. A cold wind howled around them.

'I think we should keep together and fly low,' said Regal. 'It's our best chance to find her.' They took off in formation and crossed the border. Regal was slightly ahead of the others as they skimmed across the ground. She was aiming to land by a river bank when she suddenly came to a halt. The others followed. They were all suspended in mid-air.

'What's happening? I can't move,' said Jax.

'It's... I don't know. What is this stuff, it's horrible,'s aid Madeleine, trying to wipe off the sticky transparent liquid that was covering her arms and face. 'Help me!' But there was no help because Regal and Jax were also covered in the liquid. All of them, trapped inside giant bubbles that drifted into the air.

'Try and burst the bubble,' shouted Regal. But the others couldn't hear. They could only see her mouth moving. They tried pushing against the sides but nothing worked. The bubbles were drifting higher and higher, being blown about in the wind. Jax tried punching the sides but It felt like the bubbles were made of the toughest steel. Coral reached for her special laser torch, and waved it above her head, so that the others could see. Coral, what a genius! thought Jax I knew she'd find a way out! But the laser beam didn't work either. It just bounced off the bubble wall. Even Regal, who never panicked and always remained calm, looked worried. There was no way out and no chance of finding Willow now.

11

Mr Dodakin

'I can't do this all over again, I just can't. I want to go home, get somebody else, please..please you know I'm not trained. Why aren't you coming for me Regal? Jax?' Thought you were my friends.' There was no answer. I stumbled on, not having a clue where I was going. But I knew that's exactly what I had to do-keep going.

The sounds were changing. I could smell the sea. I was no longer in a meadow. I could hear waves gently lapping on the shore. I was on a beach. I slipped off my trainers and paddled in the water. Looking round I could just make out something very white in front of me, glistening on the sand. I tapped my new stick and then walked straight into a building, smacking my face against the wall.

'What are you trying to do, you silly girl, demolish my house?' said a man's voice.

'I'm sorry, I didn't see it,' I said licking my lips. 'Sugar? I can taste sugar,'

'Of course you can! That's what my house is made of. Sugar cubes. I built it myself. It's in the shape of a pyramid. So don't try knocking it down, or eating it, thank you very much!'

'Sorry, I didn't realise.'

'So what do you want? I'm a very busy person.'

'Can you help me? I'm a Ramshackle warrior trying to find Birdgirl. She maybe in trouble. I've come from Barley meadow and I don't know how I got here. Do you know her?'

'Maybe I do. Maybe I don't. I am the official recorder of all things and all people. Nothing leaves here or moves from this beach unless I say so. In the name of Sebastian Archibald Dodikin, that's me, I hereby give notice that I refuse to let you pass.'

I tried to picture in my mind what this strange man looked like. I imagined that he wore a lime green jacket and orange trousers and a cap of red felt.

'No no, no, NO! I've decided. You don't look like a warrior. You could be lying, you could be telling me porky pies.'

'I am not lying! It's really important, Mr Doddery!'

'Dodikin!'

'Sorry, Mr Dodikin, I need to find Birdgirl. I think she can help me get back to Ramshackle house,' I said slipping against the sugary cube house.

'Oh, do be careful,wretched girl!'

'Stop shouting at me! It's not my fault that I can't see and I think you are a very rude man. I might make mistakes but I never speak to people like that!'

'Ooo..' said Dodikin, lowering his voice, 'I didn't realise, sorry. But I need to ask you some questions before I let you pass. First question, how many fish live in the sea?'

'I don't know,' I said.

'Have a guess,' said Mr Dodikin.

'Mmm.. two million?'

'Wrong. No fish live in the Dead sea, that's why they call it the Dead Sea, silly.'

'You didn't say the Dead sea.'

'Yes I did! And you better get this question right. What's the difference between an elephant and a tiger?'

'An elephant has a trunk and a tiger is a big cat with orange and black stripes who lives in the jungle.'

'Wrong again, a tiger lives in the sea but an elephant doesn't.'

'Tigers don't live in the sea!' said Willow.

'A sea tiger does.'

'Now you're being silly!'

'I don't think you know anything about our Earth and you're not on my collection list,' said Dodikin.

'I do know lots about the Earth. I'm named after a tree. I have a garden at home and I grow radishes and I made a den with my friends Sam and Ella last summer, before I joined the Ramshackles.

'What is your tree name then? Fir, oak sycamore?'

'My name's Willow, and I really do need to go. I don't suppose you have seen any of my Ramshackle friends, looking for me?'

'No. Not seen anyone. Not for a million years. But I need to check you out before I give permission for you to pass through my beach.'

I heard Dodikin move over to the side of his cube house and tap one of the bricks. 'We will see if you are telling the truth. Find me Willow and her friend Salmonella in the den.'

'No, it's Sam and Ella not salmonella!'

'All right, all right, I've got it,' he said, tapping his fingers across the slab like a keyboard. At once the slab turned into a giant screen. And I could see it in my mind so clearly.

'Wow! How did you do that?'

'Look carefully,' said Mr Dodikin.

'I can see something,' I said, 'this is cool.' The

screen flickered in front of me. Images were coming into focus. And there I was going down the slope into our den, passing the bush of brambles into our special hiding place at the bottom. 'It's my den!' It is! I know it is. Look, there's our see -saw we made, that was Sam's idea and Ella...oh, there they are!' Sam and Ella sat on a log, drinking tea out of tiny china cups. 'Oh, wow! Sam and Ella. I can see Sam and Ella!' I screamed jumping in the air. 'We used to go there after school every day, we're the only ones allowed to join. It's a secret club, hidden away in the trees so no one else knows where it is. Not even the Ramshackles. We've got a table where we have picnics and we have even put in a toilet. See, that's what those stones with a circle in the middle are used for.'

'A stone toilet? In a den? Quite remarkable, never heard anything like it,' said Mr Dodikin.

'It's quite a steep drop to get in and last year Sam's granddad came to look at our den and he slipped. Sam tried to help him but he fell right down into a ditch.'

'He's obviously a very clumsy man,' said Dodikin.

'It was an accident but Ella grabbed his arm and pulled him out,' said Willow.

'Ella pulled his arm off? She's not a very good rescuer.'

'No, he was fine but we decided to put in some steps so if he comes again he won't fall down.' For a moment I thought about the fun we had in that lovely den.

The image then changed to show a garden with lettuces and radishes growing in lines, 'My nature garden at Ramshackle House! It's still there. I need to water them.' I stopped speaking as the image faded away. And I knew where I wanted to be.

'I can see all this makes you sad, but I will help you,' said Mr Dodikin.

'How did you do that? How could I see my friends when I can't see them when I'm there?'

'It's a temporary thing, the images don't last but

you can see them in your head. I will record that you have been here and give you permission to access my beach.'

'Thank you, thank you, Mr Dodikin, can you tell me if I'm going the right way? Will I find Birdgirl?'

'There's never a right way. Yes, you will find Birdgirl but trust me, keep away from the wicked land or else the bad monster Orcusa will find you. But be very careful. And don't fall over the the edge of the world. That's where the sea meets the sky. Do you know what will happen to you if you fall off the edge of the world? First they say you will enter a sea of boiling blood and then monsters will devour you before tipping you over the edge. Best of luck.' And with that Mr Dodakin was gone. The sugar cube house crumbled all around me until nothing was left.

I felt a message in the palm of my hand.

Step in the boat, be on your way,
soon you will find her, Come what may...

12

The Edge of the World

Ouch! I stubbed my toe straight into something wooden, blocking my way. I felt my way around. Is this the boat ? I stepped into it and nearly lost my balance. I was no longer on the beach but bobbing up and down on the water. There was no garden on the other side. I was surrounded by water. It wasn't really a boat. I was standing on a raft made of several logs with a small sail that flapped in a gentle breeze. There was hardly room for me to stand up. I did find a wooden paddle at my feet. 'What am I supposed to do with this?' I said out loud. The only time I had been on a boat before was on a lake in an amusement park, one of those boats you have to pedal. I remember going round and round in circles and my friends laughing. But this was no boating lake. I was in the middle of the ocean, surrounded by water on all sides. No other boats, no buildings, no people.

Regal, I don't know where to go. Someone help me. I tried to concentrate very hard to see if I could pick up her thoughts. All I could hear were the gentle waves slapping against the side of the raft. Where am I supposed to go next? I waited. No answer. I don't like being on the water, it makes me feel sick.

'AAAHHRRG' a horrible screech pierced the silent ocean. Must be a gull, not a shark, I hope. Then it started to rain. Heavy spots stung my face. There was nowhere to shelter, just a flimsy canvas sail. But as the wind blew stronger the little raft moved much faster in the water. The waves were now crashing over the side of the raft, drenching me with ice cold, salty water. Trying to paddle was useless now. All I could do was cling on to the mast and hope for the best. So frightened.

I could feel each giant wave rising up before me like a grey, foamy mountain, tipping the little raft up and down. I was certain I was about to capsize. And above the roaring wind I could hear laughter. Gruesome laughter. Something was moving very fast behind me, surfing the waves and getting ever closer, blowing the wind even fiercer. Then a voice, so close I thought somebody was on the raft with me. 'Welcome,' it croaked in my ear, 'to the Edge of the World. You are doomed!'

There was no way I could steer the raft. I was shaking as the raft hurtled down at great speed, completely out of control. I clung to the mast so tightly I could feel slivers of wood piercing my fingers. Suddenly, there was a loud crack and the raft split in two, throwing me into the wall of foaming water. There was nothing to hold onto now. I was going down faster and faster. I knew I wouldn't survive. And the horrible voice still screaming in my head. 'You failed!'

But instead of crashing on rocks at the bottom, I was going up again. Something or someone was lifting me up and out of the waterfall. I landed with a bump on my back and lay on the ground, trying to get my breath back. And I could feel the sun on my face.

'Not a good idea to fall over the edge of the world,' said a voice beside me.

'Ouch!.ouch! I don't think..I ever...ever..ever want to go on a boat again, I'm covered in bruises,' I said, sitting up and rubbing my arms. 'Did you save me?'

'Yes. I happened to be patrolling the area and I just knew someone was in trouble.'

'Thank you, thank you so much. I don't suppose you're Birdgirl are you?'

'Yes, I am.'

'Because I've spent all this time looking for - WHAT! You really are Birdgirl?' I scrambled up beside her. 'You're joking me!'

'I'm Birdgirl.'

I reached out and grabbed her arm,

'Wow! I've been looking for you for ages! Hey, I thought you might have wings, being called Birdgirl.'

'I am Mya-Rose, Princess of the sky. I'm known as Birdgirl because I look after all the birds on Earth, but I'm not a bird myself.'

'But you can fly?'

'Yes, and I am going to teach you how to fly.'

'I won't be able to. I can't see very well, some days I can't see anything at all. I'd be hopeless.'

'No, you won't, But first come inside and have some lemon drizzle cake.'

Inside was an amazing little house, except it was perfectly round and the walls were made of twigs woven together. 'Wow, this is a birds nest!' I laughed, having explored all the way round before sitting down on a soft carpet.

We ate the cake and I told Mya-Rose all about my big mistake at Ramshackle House. And about all my adventures since I stepped into the transportation hub. And how the other Ramshackles were worried they hadn't heard anything from her. But now everything would be all right and Birdgirl would be able to get me home.

'It's not as simple as that. You need to learn how to fly first, especially if you're going to be a proper Ramshackle warrior. Also, the communication link has broken, I can't get it back again. So I won't be able to tell them you're OK.'

'Yeah, but you will be able to get me back home again?'

'Hope so. But there's another problem. Orcusa. A demon from another dimension. Sometimes he visits the land of the Wicked Way. I can feel his presence. I know he's back. I think he may be blocking our signals.'

'I've heard of him, but he's not coming here is he?'

'Hope not, finish the cake and it will be time for your first flying lesson.'

Even though I'd flown on Martin's back and walked a tightrope, I was really scared about flying on my own up in the sky. With no wings.

'No worries, first a little warm up, then you can see why I'm called Birdgirl.'

We walked through a meadow of forget-menots and buttercups, a gentle breeze rustling the hedgerow.

'It's so lovely,' I said, 'bit like my garden at home.'

'Listen.' said Mya-Rose, 'What can you hear?'

'Er..Nothing.'

'And now?'

Cuckoo Cuckoo Cuckoo

'A cuckoo! He must be over there. Arghh!' Feathers fluttered in my face as the bird landed with a thud on my shoulder.

'It's OK, he won't hurt you,' laughed Mya-Rose, who stretched out her arm for the cuckoo.

'Never been so close to a cuckoo before, what does he look like?'

'He's got like zebra stripes underneath him and crazy yellow eyes with a black dot in the middle.'

Mya-Rose lifted her arm and the cuckoo flew off heading for the trees.

'Listen again.'

'I know. Blackbird.'

'Correct.'

The hedgerow came alive with sparrows shrieking at each other and in the tree above I could hear a woodpecker drilling his beak into the the trunk.

'Hold your hand out, there's another one coming.'

The bird landed in the palm of my hand. I could tell it was a robin by its call.

'You're good at this,' said Birdgirl.

'I get a lot of practise sitting in the garden.'

Two little birds circled my head. I wasn't sure but I guessed goldfinches by their song. And I was right.

'There's a barn owl flying in now.'

He landed on my shoulder and I stroked his back.

'I love owls, he's gorgeous, I want one!'

'This one's a she, her name's Dawn.'

High in the sky there came a high pitched hissing from the swifts. The chirping, the shrills, the squawks and the squeals became so loud that for a moment I had to cover my ears. Gradually, the sounds subsided.

'Now I know why they call you Birdgirl!'

'OK. What about this call?" said Mya-Rose.

In the distance I could hear a low squawking .

'Any idea?'

'Not sure, maybe starlings?'

'Yes! Well done.'

'They do this murmuration thing, they make patterns in the sky. Coral told me all about them. Of course, I've never seen them but Coral says there are thousands of them.'

'Loads of people have seen a murmuration. But nobody's done what you are going to do.'

'What's that?'

'Fly in the middle of them.'

'No, I can't do that. I'm not ready.'

'Stand still, arms out straight. That's it. When I say go, just push up on your toes and tip yourself forward, like getting ready to do a dive in the pool. Don't worry, I'll be with you, you can't fall. So ready, steady, Go!'

I tipped forward slowly and a second later I

was propelled into the air. And there I was up in the sky flying alongside Mya-Rose in the middle of a million starlings! The noise of their beating wings was like an express train. In the middle of one group, I felt a fantastic rush of air on my face as the force of the birds pulled me towards the ground before soaring up again. It was the most exciting roller coaster I had ever been on! And I knew I was safe as Mya-Rose was right beside me. She said the birds were dancing a ballet in the sky. Mya- Rose showed me how to make a left turn in the air by dropping my arm slightly, like giving a hand signal. It was amazing, I could feel the birds all around me, very close, their feathers brushing my hands and my face but not once did we collide. Mya-Rose shouted that the birds were forming different shapes in the sky, first a giant swan and then a snake with a tail! Gradually, I felt the movement of the birds was slowing down. As the starlings disappeared in their thousands, Mya-Rose and I floated gently over a lake before landing back in the meadow. I couldn't say anything.

'You OK?' said Mya-Rose, waving a hand in front of my face.

'That was the most beautiful thing I've ever done in my life,' I said. 'Wow! It was amazing. How did you do that? Are you a magician?'

'No, I'm not a magician, the magic's all around us. We just have to look for it,' said Mya-Rose. 'That's why they call me Birdgirl. I wanted you to experience something beautiful.'

'I did! I did! It was totally awesome.'

'Glad you liked it, Willow. Would you like another go?'

'Yes, please! Are we flying with the starlings again?'

'No, a bit further this time.'

Instantly I felt the the sky darken.

'There, on the Eastern horizon, is Venus,' said Mya-Rose. 'They call it the Evening Star, although it's not actually a star, it's a planet. Hold tight. We're going there now!'

13

The Evening Star

Mya-Rose and I hurtled into the sky. We passed into a   corridor of green light, heading towards Venus. There was blackness all around but I could see this band of light that we were travelling through. As we got nearer, the planet changed to a fiery orange ball.

'I can see! I can see, it's like a giant tangerine,' I joked, enjoying the ride and feeling perfectly safe holding on to Mya-Rose's arm. 'Look, it's turning pink and blue now. Wow! What a beautiful planet. Can't believe I'm going to Venus!' But then without warning, the planet completely disappeared and the view was replaced by a thick, grey fog. 'Can't see anything now.'

'It's OK, we're going down.' Through the

clouds we floated and I could just make out the land coming up very fast to meet us. We landed together on both feet.

'It's a shame it's so foggy today,' I said, 'I wish I could see the orange and purple colours again.'

'It's not fog, it's a whole load of poisonous gases. It's what the atmosphere is made of here,' said Mya-Rose.

I pinched my nose 'We'll get poisoned!'

'No, we won't, we are protected by a bubble. You can't see it, but it's keeping out all the gases. Nothing can harm us here.'

'I was expecting Venus to be beautiful, they say it shines so bright in the sky, but it's awful. Can't see a thing.' I knelt down and ran my hand through the soil, it felt like soft sand. I let the grains pour though my fingers. Then the ground started to vibrate and a heavy clanking noise filled the air. The fog around us suddenly lifted.

The land was covered in filthy buildings, some of which had giant wheels revolving at the side, others with massive hammers that smashed repeatedly into the ground. But all of them had chimneys protruding into the sky, belching thick smoke.

'Are these factories?'

'Yes, mining for metals,' said Mya-Rose.

'Are there people inside?'

'Hardly any, it's all automatic. No prizes for guessing who did all this. Orcusa took control of this planet years ago. He loves metal. And these factories poison the air. Don't worry, as I told you, we're not breathing this stuff in.'

'Does this Orcusa live here?' I don't like the sound of him at all.'

'No, we're OK. He's not here. Come on, if we walk further away from the factories we can reach the sea, just over the next hill.'

'Yay! I love the sea!' I was expecting the ground to be rocky and hard but it was quite soft to walk on. We climbed up a gentle slope and Mya-Rose stopped.

'There. The sea. Come and look, Willow.' But there was nothing there. I could just make out huge grey lumps of dried mud and clay that stretched into the distance.

'This is a joke, right?'

'No, not a joke, it's the truth. Once this was a vast ocean. Venus had many oceans and underground lakes but they all dried up. The temperature became so hot and with the poisonous clouds it killed everything.' I took a couple of steps onto the uneven blocks, scared I might fall over.

'Did it have fish?'

'Yep, sadly, all wiped out. You can find bones and skeletons though if you look hard enough.'

'It's horrible, I want to go back.'

'We will. But I've got one more thing to show you,' said Mya-Rose, turning back to the factory area. 'Over there.' At the end of a line of factories there was an enormous tip that towered into the sky. Several conveyor belts linked to the factory buildings carried lumps of rock and soil and then shunted them on to the tip.

'Mining. All the stuff churned up from the

ground is thrown on the tip and then it gets sorted by the children.'

'CHILDREN! You mean people live here!'

At first I thought it was a pack of animals but as we got nearer to the base of the tip, I could see a group of children. Not very old, maybe six or seven years. They were dressed in ragged clothes, clambering over the mounds and sifting through piles of jagged metal.

'Orcusa uses them as slave labour to find precious metals for himself. Apart from a few guards no one else lives here.'

'But I thought you said no one could live here because of the poisoned air?'

'These are not children from Earth. Orcusa has sent them here to work. They come from another planet.'

'Can we ..can we talk to them ?' I said, thinking I was going to cry.

'They can't see us or here us, we are just observers, like being in a little bubble. They wouldn't understand us. Now it's time for us to return.'

Back where we started. 'Why did you take me there? It's horrible. Those poor children, why can't you do something about it?'

'I can't. I wish I could. But it's a different dimension, we can only observe for a short time. Venus is Earth's twin. It was once a beautiful planet until Orcusa got his hands on it. And if we don't stop Orcusa, who knows what he might do to our planet.' I blew out my cheeks and wiped an arm across my face.

'Venus is what our Earth could be like in years to come. That's why we have to stop Orcusa before it's too late. And who knows, maybe even Venus will be beautiful again if we get rid of Orcusa,' said Mya-Rose.

We finished off the lemon drizzle cake. My vision was very hazy. I could just about make out cups and plates, but it was so much better than it was before I left Ramshackle house. And yet when I was on Venus I wished I couldn't see.

'Thank you, thank you so much, Mya-Rose. I shall never forget flying with the birds. You are the most amazing girl I've ever met. Now I'm ready to go home.'

'It's gone,' said Mya-Rose, 'it's gone!'

'What's gone?

'My precious emerald, I always keep it hidden in this box buried in the ground. It's not there.'

'Is it valuable'

'It's my life. My birthstone. Without it I have no power.'

I jumped up. 'Don't worry I'll help you look for it, must be here somewhere.'

'It's not here. I know where it is. There's a note in the box. "Hahha, missing something? Come and get it if you dare! "' She held up the note. 'It's signed Orcusa the Great.'

'What will you do?'

Mya-Rose took some time before she answered. 'I don't have a choice, I am nothing without the emerald. I will have to go and get it back.'

14

All the Birds have Flown

Mya-Rose rushed outside. I stumbled behind her.

'Listen', she said. 'What can you hear?'

'Nothing.'

'Exactly. Nothing. There are no birds in the sky, no birds singing. They've all gone. Orcusa is controlling them now. I'm really sorry, Willow, I can't get you home or fly very far without the emerald. You'll have to stay here till I return.'

'No way, I'm coming with you. And that's the end of it.'

'I'll have to go through the tunnels in the land of the Wicked Way, it's very dangerous. Willow, it's too risky. I need to go now.'

I grabbed her arm. 'I'm not staying here. I'm

coming with you and that's it. We will do this together.'

'All right. But we'll have to walk.'

And so with Mya-Rose leading the way we walked over scrub land and bumpy ground. The beautiful flower meadow became a field of brambles and weeds until at last we came to a halt. The mouth of a cave.

'This is it. This is the underground entrance to Orcusa's castle. Are you sure you want to do this?' said Mya-Rose. She read out the sign above the entrance

Welcome to the tunnels of Dread

But it wasn't that dreadful, not to start with. The tunnel was wide enough for us to walk side by side. We stopped for a rest. Mya- Rose wasn't saying very much. I could tell she was worried about the loss of her emerald stone.

I sat down beside her. 'Do you know what Orcusa looks like?' I said.

'No, I don't.'

'Only I think I may have seen him.'

'How come?'

'I mean, like an image in my mind. Once when I was on the tightrope at the circus, and then again, he chased me when I was on the sea in that boat. It was horrible, he was like a grey blob with a massive slit for a mouth. He tried to make me fall off the wire and I nearly did. And then he pushed me over the edge of the world before you rescued me. It was so real. You must have seen him.'

'He wasn't there, it was probably a mirage, you imagined him. That can be really frightening,' said Mya-Rose.

I tried to get the image of Orcusa out of my mind. But I couldn't. I started to tremble and I could feel my heart thumping in my chest.'

'Are you OK?' said Mya-Rose.

'Yeah, I'll be all right in a minute.'

'I guess we shall find out what he looks like very soon. We are now in the tunnels of Dread, Orcusa's territory. We are getting closer and closer.'

'Do you think he knows we're here? I said, sitting up.

'I'm sure he does.'

I picked up a broken stick and made patterns in the dry, dusty ground. All the while I was getting more and more upset. 'I can't do this anymore,' I said, 'I want to go back. I quit. I'm really sorry, Mya- Rose. I can't help you.'

'Hey, ' said Mya-Rose sitting beside me, 'It will be all right. Listen, I need you Willow. You're so brave.'

Then it all came tumbling out 'I'm not brave, I'm a weakling. I can't do anything properly, I can't throw, I can't run, the only thing I can catch is a cold. And I can't see. I'm useless.'

'Not true,' said Mya-Rose.

'I cheated on sports day,' I said, digging the stick harder into the ground.

'What?'

'I cheated. Supposed to be doing the egg and spoon race, it's the only event they put me in every year. My egg always falls off the spoon and I come last. And so this year I cheated. I got a golf ball and stuck it on a spoon with glue and kept it in my bag until my race. No one knew, so we all lined up. Ready, steady Go! And the gun went off. I tore down the track. Everyone was jumping up and down and calling out my name and that had never happened before.'

'So, you won the race and now you feel guilty?' said Mya-Rose.

'No, I didn't win the race. I was winning and only about one meter away from the tape. Huh. Guess what? Then I tripped over and fell, and everyone else passed me. And I came last, as usual.'

Mya-Rose burst out laughing.

'What's so funny?' You're laughing because I fell over. I know I can't do anything right. That's why they don't want me to be a Ramshackle.'

'No, Willow, I'm not laughing because you fell over. I'm thinking here is a girl who walked a deadly tightrope over a waterfall, who's defied Orcusa all the way, flown on a giant bee, saved a bee colony, stood up against the bullies, sailed on a raft, and fell off the edge of the world! And you've been to Venus and flown with the birds in the sky. And you think the egg and spoon race is the most important thing in your life.'

I must admit I had to smile, before we both laughed out loud.

'But I am so scared now, I can't do this. I was terrified on the raft and on the tightrope. And when Orcusa's face appeared, I nearly fell.'

'But you didn't. Willow, it's OK to feel scared, even the bravest heroes get scared. That's what makes you strong. Willow, I need you by my side. I can't do this without you.'

'Do you mean that?'

'Of course I do. It's Orcusa, his power stretches down this tunnel, he's messing with our minds. I want my birds back, I want my world back. If we stop now it's over. Trapped in these caves. Forever. And you Willow, will never see Ramshackle House again..'

I sat with my head in my hands for some time

and then I leapt up.

'Yes, I will!' I shouted. 'Bring it on, Orcusa!' I started chopping the air and aiming high karate kicks at an imaginary opponent. 'This is how to do it. I've done a bit of karate. He doesn't scare me and there's two of us now. You can zap him to Jupiter or somewhere, Mya-Rose. We'll show him. Girl power. Yay!' I raised my fist in salute.

'This is Orcusa's domain,' said Mya-Rose.

'Yeah, you said.'

'Listen. I don't have any power here, none at all. I can't zap him to Jupiter or anywhere else. I wish it could be different,' said Mya-Rose. 'But I know one thing. You're ready now, and I promise I'll stay with you whatever happens. We'll do this together.'

Sometimes friends don't need words to express how they feel. I smiled and linked arms with Mya-Rose. The final and most dangerous journey had begun.

15

The Tunnels of Dread

'They are in the tunnels,' said Orcusa.

'Yes,my lord, I smell them, I smell them!'

'Let's hope they can't smell you, Ludo.'

'My lord, let me get at them, please pretty please,' begged Ludo, jumping and twitching in the air. 'It's my turn, it's my turn.'

'No, because you'll eat them, and part of me wants to meet this weeping Willow, before I dispose of her.'

'I want to eat her as well! Sorry, I mean meet her as well.'

'There's two of them. Weepy Willow and her friend, Birdygirl. The goddess of birds or something on Earth. I hate birds, horrible feathery things, always screeching, weak pathetic creatures, just like this Birdygirl,' said Orcusa. 'We will see how good she is now her power has gone, Ha!'

'I eat birds,' said Ludo.

'No, Ludo, you can meet them in the tunnel, scare them real bad. But bring them to me alive. Alive, do you understand? Alive!'

'Yes, my lord, I will do what you command.' Ludo scuttled away, a huge grin forming around his crooked, broken teeth.

Mya-Rose and I reached a point where the trail we had been following branched into three tunnels.

'So which way do we go?' I said. Stretching out my arms I could touch the walls and the roof.

'The tunnel to the left is marked with a sign that says *Warning Dead End. Highly Dangerous. DO NOT ENTER,*' said Mya-Rose. 'The one to the right is marked with an arrow saying *This is the Right Way.* Doesn't say anything about the tunnel straight ahead.'

I looked down at the palm of my hand again, hoping that there might be a clue which passage to take. There was nothing. From the tunnels came a soft groaning.

'What's that?' I said.

'Probably just the wind, ' said Mya-Rose, 'quite common underground.'

'So we go right, yeah? I said.

'Why do you say that?' said Mya-Rose.

'I'm not going down the other one, you said it was highly dangerous. And this one says this is the right way.'

'Maybe it's a trick. Maybe they want us to go right, but the real way, the correct way is to the left,' said Mya-Rose. 'Or we could go straight on. There's no sign on that one.'

'Or we could just go back,' I said.

'Shh! Listen. Can you hear it?'

High pitched shrieks were coming from deep inside the tunnel and getting louder. I put my hands over my ears. 'It's horrible, what is it?'

The ground started to vibrate beneath us.

'Something is coming round the next bend,' said Mya-Rose, 'a wild horse by the sound of it and he's coming very fast.'

'A horse!' I said, 'What are we going to do, there's no room-'

Before we had time to move the thing hurtled round the bend and skidded to a halt a few feet away, showering me with dust. I pressed myself against the tunnel wall and wiped the dust from my eyes. I clung on to Mya-Rose's arm. 'What is it?' I whispered, 'It doesn't smell like a horse.'

'It's not a horse, it's a rat!' she screamed, 'A giant rat!'

16

Meeting Ludo

A rush of his stinking breath, a mixture of poo and garlic, almost choked us in the tunnel. Mya-Rose was gently tugging my sleeve and moving backwards, 'Be cool, no sudden movements, he don't look very friendly.'

'How big is he?' I whispered, 'is he really a giant?' I could hear the rat clicking his teeth together and I imagined a blood red tongue, dripping saliva, darting between yellow, jagged teeth. Turns out that I was right.

'Leaving so soon, you're wasting your time trying to escape. There's no way out,' said Ludo, his head moving closer, 'my lord wants to meet you. He said I should bring you both alive but I want to eat you, but he said "No,no, no, no". So I promised him I wouldn't eat you. But he's not here is he? So that's exactly what I am going to do. Eat you. Not sure which one of you I shall munch on first.' His head bobbed from side to side, 'Girlybird or weepy Willow!'

Now's the time for me to show Ramshackle courage. I strode forward and pointed a finger at where I thought the rat was standing.

'Nice try ratty, but you don't exist. I've worked it out, you're just one of those mirage things.'

'Willow! No!' shrieked Mya-Rose.

'You don't frighten me. So shoo, go away, you little pest.'

Ludo bared his teeth and moved forward.

'I don't think he is a mirage,' said Mya-Rose.

'Of course he is, we just stand here and wait for him to disappear,' I said, smiling.

'Or we could just.. RUN!' said Mya-Rose. As Ludo lurched forward we turned and sprinted down the passage. I could feel Ludo lumbering not far behind, his foul breath getting closer. Mya-Rose and I were running so fast she didn't see which way we were going. And at the crossroads we hurtled into another tunnel, the tunnel marked *'Dead End.'*

'I have you now,' cackled Ludo, 'it's a dead end, or in your case, it's two dead ends,' he cackled.

'We picked the wrong one. There's no way out ,' said Mya-Rose. 'Get behind this rock, it's our only chance.' I bent down and picked up a stone from the floor.

'I'm coming, ready or not,' said Ludo, moving slowly down the tunnel, his nose and whiskers twitching. 'I can smell you. Come out, come out wherever you are!'

I sensed him getting nearer and nearer. I flung the pebble as hard as I could and heard the crack as it smacked his nose. He uttered a piercing cry that screeched off the tunnel walls. For a moment, I felt sorry for hurting him. He was really mad now. And coming straight for me. I turned and ran down the tunnel. Mya-Rose was waiting for me behind a rock in the tunnel wall. She grabbed my arm and pulled me though a very narrow gap.

Only just in time. Ludo was close behind, moving very fast. He caught our scent as he came level with the rock where we were hiding. But he had forgotten one thing. The tunnel got narrower and narrower. Ludo was running so fast he couldn't stop until his body became jammed between the two sides of the tunnel.

'I know where you are,' he said, 'I'll have you, just you wait.' But he was stuck fast. He tried wriggling backwards, he tried kicking up dust, but the sharp pieces of rock sticking into his sides held him even more firmly in place.

'At least his head's up the other end,' said Mya-Rose. 'He's not going anywhere and while he's stuck we can get away.' But unfortunately Ludo was stuck right in front of us. A mountain of thick, matted, grey fur that blocked the tunnel from roof to ceiling.

'But how can we?' I said.

'There's only one thing we can do,' said Mya-Rose, 'climb through his fur and over his back.'

Ludo howled and squealed as Mya-Rose and I

started to climb up the side of the giant rat. I found it hard to cling on. Ludo's fur was so greasy and I kept losing my grip. Although he couldn't move forward or backwards, Ludo shook his body and arched his back trying to shake us off. Somehow I managed to hold on. Mya-Rose reached the top of Ludo's back and I was right behind her. This is where it became difficult because we had to squeeze into the tiny gap between Ludo and the tunnel roof, which meant pressing our faces down into Ludo's stinking fur. As we tried to pull ourselves across his back, I held my breath and kept my mouth tightly closed as I felt Ludo's prickly fur on my face. Maggots wriggled on my lips and fleas crawled up my face and bit my cheeks. I wanted to scream but I daren't open my mouth.

'Get off me!' yelled Ludo, 'You will pay for this.' After what seemed to be a lifetime crawling through the forest of Ludo's stinking fur, we found the curve in his back and managed to slide down onto the ground.

'Watch his tail!' said Mya-Rose. The tail lashed the ground like a whip, whistling inches away from my face.

'Lets get out of here while we still can,' said Mya-Rose.

'That was the most disgusting thing I've ever done in my life,' I said 'I always thought fur was meant to be soft and cuddly, like my cat Suki.'

'Guess you haven't cuddled too many giant rats. Hey, Willow, you were brilliant in there, that was so brave.'

'Yeah, well, I nearly missed our hiding place. Luckily, you grabbed me, otherwise stinky whiskers would have had me for lunch. Makes me feel sick just thinking about it.'

We hurried along the tunnel. 'I guess if we go this way we must be getting close to Orcusa's fortress,' said Mya-Rose.

The path became much steeper as if we were climbing an underground hill. When we reached the top the path became level again. Mya-Rose stopped.

'What is it? Not another rat I hope!'

'No. There's a massive gate ahead and it's open. This is too easy, could be a trick,' said Mya-Rose.

'Orcusa must know we're here,' I said, walking on, feeling the sides of the tunnel.

'Hey, hang on.'

The ground beneath our feet started to shake. Clouds of hot steam hissed and sprouted from below like a giant kettle on the boil.

'Come back, Willow! I think it's an earthquake!'

But before I could take another step I could feel the ground in front of me cracking and tearing apart. I was standing on the edge of a cliff. Mya-Rose could see what I couldn't see. Below me, a roaring river of orange lava was moving up very fast. I could feel the heat searing my face. Mya-Rose tried to reach me. But it was too late. A massive jolt and the ground I was standing on gave way. I plunged head first over the edge.

17

Always another Way

'Nooo.!' cried Mya-Rose. She went down on her knees and crawled towards the edge, knowing that any second she too would be falling into the fire. Blinking in the fierce heat, she hardly dare look over the edge.

'Well, you took your time!' My head appeared between two bushes, only about six feet below.

'How did you manage to do that?' said Mya-Rose, above the noise of the lava flow.

'Never mind that, just get me out of here. I'm roasting alive!'

Mya-Rose inched forward and stretched out her arm.

'Here hold onto me, I'll try and pull you up.' I

grabbed her wrist and pushed my feet on the cliff face, trying to find a foot hold. Sometimes it's better not to see. Mya-Rose knew she would only have one chance. The lava was rising fast but she was determined she wasn't going to let me go.

Mya-Rose grabbed both my arms and hauled me over the top.

We staggered back along the path to safety until the ground became cooler, before collapsing together in a breathless heap.

'That was the worst one yet, I really thought it was all over,' I said.

'Lucky those bushes were there, they saved your life,' said Mya-Rose.

I squeezed her hand. 'No, the bushes didn't save my life, you did.'

After a few minutes we could feel the tunnel getting cooler. 'The lava level has gone down and the steam has cleared,' said Mya-Rose. 'The gate's still there but it's on the other side. The gap across the ravine must be like hundred feet. There's no way round.'

And above the gateway I was certain I could see the grinning image of Orcusa, taunting us.

'No point in us even trying. There's no way we can get across to the other side. And you can't fly any more. So near and yet so far away.' I put my head in my hands for a moment before looking up. 'Sorry, Regal, I did my best. You were right. I'm not good enough to be a Ramshackle. It's over. Please come and get me out of here.'

'Hey,' said Mya-Rose, lightly punching my arm, 'You're right, we can't get across the ravine and I can't fly any more. But she can!'

'What are you talking about?'

'There's always another way. Hold out your hand.' She pulled back a flap in her top pocket and pulled out a little bird and placed it in my hand.

'It's a robin! I know it is. You are a magician!' I said

'One of the wonderful things about being Birdgirl,' said Mya-Rose, as the robin hopped into the palm of her hand. 'I carry her with me everywhere.'

'She's beautiful, but how is this going to help us get across the ravine?' I said.

'The robin will give us enough power to get across. It's like having a reserve tank. But it will only last for a few minutes, so let's go.'

Mya-Rose brought the robin up close and whispered something. Immediately, the bird fluttered upwards and we followed.

'She's flying very close to the ceiling of the cave and now she's crossing the ravine,' said Mya-Rose.

'Poor little thing, I hope she doesn't get burned.'

'Don't worry, she'll be fine. She's just landed on top of the gate.'

'Wow! She did it!' I said, as we landed in front of the gate. Mya-Rose tucked the robin back inside her jacket.

Then, with a massive rumble, the red river of lava disappeared and the two sides of the ravine joined together again. And ahead, the final path that would take us straight into Orcusa's palace.

18

Goodbye Birdgirl

If this is meant to be a palace it's not a very nice one,' said Mya-Rose. She described what it was like. The walls were made of rough stone, leaking drops of foul yellow liquid, that trickled to the ground. There was no furniture and the floor was covered in sharp metal lumps. And there was no sign of life.

'Maybe we've got the wrong place,' said Mya-Rose.

'Yeah, he saw us coming and ran away.'

'ARGHHHH! Orcusa does not run away!' roared a voice from the other side of the room. I could hear him but couldn't see him.

'He's inside the wall, over there,' whispered

Mya-Rose. But when it started to move towards us we realised Orcusa wasn't inside the wall. Orcusa was the wall. His stone head filled up most of the room. My vision returned and I could see him quite clearly. And I wish I couldn't. I knew this was the figure that had haunted me on the tightrope and blew me over the edge of the world. His eyes were just dark holes, his mouth wide open with two protruding upper teeth. I could hear his tail lashing the ground behind him. And because he had no eyeballs, just empty sockets, I couldn't be certain he was looking at me.

'Weepy Willow, we meet at last.' The sound came from deep inside and he spoke without moving his lips. 'And the other one, the Birdy Girl.'

'My name's Willow, have some respect,' I said, in a squeaky voice. I felt myself trembling. Right now I was not feeling very brave.

'And I'm Mya-Rose.'

'Respect! Huh. I have no respect for you or you, birdy girl. I'm deciding how best to get rid of you both,' said Orcusa.

'I've come to get my emerald back. I know you have it.'

Orcusa dug deep into his grey belly and pulled out a stone.

'This what you looking for? ' Before either of us could move he thrust it back in again. 'You see Birdy girl you have no power without your so called magic stone. And I didn't steal it. You were very careless and Ludo found it.'

'Its mine and I want it back. It's part of the universal plan.'

'Really? Well, let me show you something Miss Princess of the sky.'

The ground vibrated as Orcusa roared making Willow jump.

The side wall slid open revealing a gigantic lake outside, except you could hardly see any water. Because the lake was filled with birds. Birds of all shapes and sizes. And all of them silent. Deathly silent.

Mya- Rose gasped.

'Every bird in the world is there on my Never Ending Lake. And not one of them making a sound. No more tweeting, no more screeching, no more fluttering, horrible feathery things. All gone.'

'Let them go, they've done nothing to you,' said Mya-Rose.

'Oh, I plan to let them go. One flick of this switch,' said Orcusa, placing his hand over a control panel on the arm of this throne, 'it will pull the plug at the bottom of the Never Ending Lake. All your little feathered friends will be sucked into an eternal whirlpool, down to the very core of the Earth. And there's nothing you can do about it What do you think of that Birdy girl.'

'You're horrible and you're cruel, I hate you!' I shrieked, 'just you wait till the Ramshackles arrive and see what you've done. You'll pay for this.'

Mya- Rose tried to hold back tears of anger.

'You'll kill them all,' she said, 'You really are an evil monster.'

'I'm not a monster. I'm just removing an annoying group of useless, feathery things. I'm doing the world a favour. Much better off without them.

'They do lovely things,' I said

'Such as?'

'They sing and they make people happy and they help pollinate the flowers and they have lived on this planet for about two million years.' I just guessed the last bit, I didn't know how long birds have been on this planet.

'I don't care. I want to get rid of them. And nothing can stop me. '

'I will, I'll stop you.'

Mya-Rose tried to pull me back. Orcusa rose from his throne and slithered towards us. 'What are you going to do Weepy Willow, hit me with your stick?' I grabbed the first thing I could get hold of, a jug on the table and hurled it at Orcusa. But I missed and it shattered against the wall.

'Ooo.. I'm shaking with fear. Little Weepy willow who can't see properly and Birdy Girl who has no power.' He rubbed his hands together. 'But I am a merciful leader. I will make you an offer

Birdy Girl.'

He slithered forward again as we moved back. 'Instead of sucking the birds down the plug hole in the Never Ending Lake, I'm going to let you fly them to the planet Viduka, instead. Everyone of them, out of my way for good, including you. None of you will be coming back.'

'But Viduka's a hostile planet and they won't survive the journey. It's millions of miles away.'

'Not my problem, they'll have to learn to survive. Anyway, I'm giving you a chance. You need to decide now,' said Orcusa.

I turned to Mya-Rose. 'We don't have a choice. Let's do this together, at least some of the birds might make it, better than seeing them all drown in the lake.'

'You're not coming,' said Mya-Rose, quietly.

'Yes I am! You try and stop me! You can help me fly, I'll be OK. I'm not leaving you on your own, not after what we've been through together. Besides, I don't want to stay here and-'

'No, you don't understand, Willow. I can't take

you. I don't have enough power left. Without my emerald flying stone, I'm nothing. And you will die out there.' She turned to face Orcusa, 'All right, I'll take the birds if you promise to let Willow go.'

'Maybe I will, maybe I won't. That's not your problem. The countdown is starting. Birdygirl, the plug will be pulled in ten, nine, eight, seven, six...five.

'Go! Go now!' I shouted, 'I'll be all right.'

Mya-Rose hesitated for a moment. 'I'll find a way to let you know when I arrive. Hope we meet again one day in happier times.' We hugged for the last time. I watched with tears running down my face as she hurled herself through the giant window and flew towards the lake. Although I couldn't see very much, seconds later the rush of wind and the flapping of feathers almost blew me off my feet as millions of birds all rose together in the sky and flew away in total silence.

'You sentimental little Earthlings,' laughed Orcusa, 'fancy sacrificing her own life for the stupid birds.'

It was some time before I answered. 'What do you mean?'

'There's no way she can make it to Viduka on her own. Without the power of the stone, she's done for. And Birdy girl knows it. She will run out of power and crash, and the birds will have to make their own way.'

'NO!' I screamed sinking to my knees.

'What are you worried about? She saved your life. Don't you realise that's why she wouldn't let you go with her? You're even more stupid than I thought, Weepy Willow.'

I felt for my stick on the ground, gritted my teeth and hurled myself at Orcusa with all my strength. For a second, I got in a couple of blows to his head and close up I could smell his fishy flesh. Then a blue flash sent me hurtling across the floor.

Winded, I pulled myself up, ready to try again.

'What a temper. It's no good, you can't fight me, Weepy Willow.

'Give me the emerald, and I'll go. I can still

reach Birdgirl, you don't have to do this. Orcusa, please ...I'm begging you,' I said, my vision getting weaker.

'I do have one idea. You can have the emerald, Weepy Willow, Providing... providing..'

'Providing what?'

'Providing you go and get it.'

19

Facing the Beast

A flick of a switch and a panel in the grey metal wall rose. Behind the panel there was a massive cage and a low growl came from inside. I could smell the animal and just make out its shape.

'OK, Weepy Willow, this is my pet. Let me introduce you to Griff. Do you know what it is?'

I shook my head.

'This is my griffin. The most fearsome creature in the universe. She knows its feeding time soon, she's getting ready for her dinner.'

Griff, of course. Like the baby griffin that I have back at Ramshackle House.

'You want me to feed your griffin her dinner?' I

can do that if you let me go.'

'No,' said Orcusa. 'nothing like that. This is a little game. See, what I want you to do is to get the emerald.' I heard a clink. 'There. I've just thrown the stone into Griffy's cage. If you want to save Birdygirl all you have to do is to go into the cage and get it back. And then you can go free. Simple.'

I hesitated for a minute then moved towards the cage and felt the cold metal bars.

'How am I supposed to get in?'

'Easy, ' said Orcusa. 'There's a little trap door at the bottom, just enough room for you to crawl through. If you dare.'

I felt my way along the bars until I reached the end. I knelt down and felt a handle and pulled. The door sprang open.

'Oh,' said Orcusa, 'you're braver than I thought, or more stupid. Off you go then. Bye, Weepy Willow.'

I only had one idea left. I crawled through into the cage and heard the trap door close behind me. The griffin was in the far corner. I could smell her, I could hear her, I could feel her presence. And right in the middle of the cage floor was the gleaming emerald, sending bands of rainbow light into the air. I had no trouble in seeing the precious stone. All I had to do was to pick it up. I crawled very slowly towards it. The griffin stirred and gave a low growl. I stopped and waited. I moved forward again. I was in reach of the emerald, my hand was about to close over it when from outside the cage Orcusa hammered against the bars. The griffin sprang up and gave a terrible roar. I felt her wings open and then smash them against the side of the bars making the cage rock. Then she moved towards me, her head crouching low. I could feel my heart pounding. She dipped her head and peered at the stone. I wanted to get out of the cage, my courage had gone. But the griffin was now blocking my way back.

'Oh, dear,' laughed Orcusa, 'what are you going to do now Weepy Willow?' But then I remembered our motto, Ramshackles never give up. And I was the only one who could save Mya-

Rose. If only I could reach the emerald. The griffin was so close now I could feel its hot breath on my face, her teeth just inches away. I was certain she was ready to pounce on me.

I didn't speak. I used my thoughts. It was my only chance. It's all right, your baby's safe. I trembled as the griffin nuzzled my shoulder and sniffed. And then I knew. She could smell the scent of her baby on me. 'Let me have the emerald and I can tell you how to find your baby.' I reached up and gently stroked the side of the griffin's face.

'Please help me save Birdgirl, please.' The griffin moved back. I am certain I heard her say 'Birdgirl.' She picked up the emerald with her tongue and dropped it in my hand.

'What's going on?' said Orcusa, 'Have you put a spell on my pet? because that won't help, you're going to-' Orcusa never finished the sentence. The griffin smashed against the bars. Metal and dust flew everywhere. The cage started to collapse all around me. I crawled out of what was left of the cage, making sure I kept hold of the emerald. I could see clearer now. The griffin was heading straight for Orcusa, who backed away. 'Go back, you horrible beast or I'll have you thrown in the lake, do you hear me? For I am Orcusa the Great, I am more powerful than any foul beast. See how you like a thunder bolt smashing your brains out.' But Orcusa never had the chance to press his control panel. The griffin grabbed him in her mouth and shook him from side to side, like a rag doll.

'Put me down, put me down,' screamed Orcusa. And then she was gone, smashing her way through the window, with Orcusa dangling from her claws. Most of the castle wall on the east side was down. I could just make out the griffin flying over the Never Ending Lake. Then I saw something falling from the sky followed by a tremendous splash. Orcusa was gone. And so was the griffin. I managed to stumble through the dust and rubble to reach what was left of the window ledge, like two hundred feet above the ground. I gripped the

the emerald stone in my hand and stretched my arms out in front of me, as if I was going to dive, like Mya-Rose taught me. And then..I couldn't do it. I felt the the ledge crumbling under my feet. I wasn't brave enough. I had used up all my courage in that cage with the griffin. 'I'm sorry Mya-Rose, I can't do it. I'm too scared,' Then I remembered her words:

'It's good to be scared, how else can we show courage?'

'You saved my life Mya-Rose, you saved my life. And now I'm going to save yours.'

20

Don't Look Down

I closed my eyes as I thought this might help then toppled forward into the sky. I tipped head first and tried really hard to keep my arms straight. My head came up and I was flying in a straight line and keeping steady. But I didn't know where I was going and how long I could manage to keep this up. Whatever you do, don't look down, Willow. It was a sudden rush of air from below that propelled me upwards. I couldn't control what I was doing and a massive cloud swept over me. I felt myself being pulled up and then dropped on something soft and furry that was moving very fast through the air.

Hold on tight, a voice told me in my head *Hold*

on tight.

You're safe now Willow, so let's go find Birdgirl! I opened my eyes a tiny bit. Griffin! I was sitting on her back with my arms clinging around her neck. It was still pretty scary hanging on as the wind made my eyes water and pounded my head. But it was a relief that I didn't have to fly. I kept my eyes closed but when I opened them again I could just make out we were flying over the ocean, an endless grey ocean with white, foamy waves. I had no idea where we were going, and for a moment I thought the griffin was taking me up to her nest. Oh, no, I'm dinner after all this!

*Birdgirl ahead...*it was such a clear thought and it was coming from the griffin. The griffin made a very sharp turn to the right. We dropped down very suddenly and then I saw her. Mya-Rose bobbing up and down on a block of ice in the middle of the ocean.

This is where she had landed after she had used up what was left of her power. The griffin flew around twice. The ice cold wind was freezing my face and fingers, I daren't let go. About fifty feet below, Mya-Rose was waving to us and trying to keep her balance. The griffin kept flying round and round....*Too big,,,can't reach...too close to waves and I crash ..we don't get up again.*

'So how are we going to get Mya-Rose, then?' I shouted above the wind. The griffin didn't answer. But I answered myself. I would have to fly down. I don't know how high up I was but I would have to try after my one and only flying lesson. *Go now...you can..use emerald stone.*

Yes, of course! All I had to do was land on the ice with Mya-Rose and give her the stone. That's all. I really didn't want to let go of griffin. I licked my frozen lips and shouted to Mya-Rose. 'I'm coming !' For once, I had to look down. It wasn't a dive, more of a tumble as I fell off griffin. But this time I kept my arms straight and flew over Mya-Rose, looking for the best spot to land. Except there wasn't one. Each time I got near I would overshoot the target, and had to go round again. I was convinced I would end up crashing in the sea.

It was like the twentieth go, I was coming in too fast and I didn't know how to slow down. Until Mya-Rose reached up and grabbed me. She pulled me down onto the ice floe beside her. There was hardly room for us to stand up.

'So pleased to see you,' I said, as Mya- Rose grabbed the emerald. She didn't reply. Seconds later we soared into the air, and headed west. Now I was much more confident flying alongside Mya-Rose. 'No time, we have to stop the birds before it's too late!' she shouted . The little robin poked her head out of Mya-Rose's pocket.

*I help...I help..*Griffin flew behind us and flapped her giant wings which produced a powerful wind that drove us forwards. We were so high up. I couldn't see the ocean anymore, but in front of us a huge storm cloud appeared.

'That's not a cloud, it's the birds!' said Mya-Rose.

We overtook the the birds and using the power of the emerald, Mya-Rose managed to turn the birds round in mid-air. Griffin did her bit finding any

143

stragglers and pointing them in the right direction. And then something wonderful happened. The birds started to sing. All around me they croaked and squeaked and sang the most beautiful songs.

'This is amazing! Mya-Rose, you've saved them all!'

'No, you did! Even though you're a useless flyer!' I think we were both crying now.

'Hey, that's harsh,' I joked. 'But you're right. I am a bit useless.'

'Willow, let's go home.'

21

The Warriors Return

And with Griffin providing the power again behind us, we soared through the sky, the land below a blur of blue and green. I was flying alongside Mya-Rose. 'I'm doing well, aren't I?' I said, just before a massive wobble.

'You're not quite ready to go solo yet,' said Mya Rose, pulling me level again. 'Whoa'! said Mya-Rose, 'Slow down.'

'What's the problem?'

'Round objects floating in the air, look like beach balls. We need to be careful. Let me go first and take a look.'

I couldn't see anything, the objects were too far away and there was a mist clinging to my eyelids.

Please don't let this be some awful trick by
Orcusa, I thought.

'I don't believe it!' said Mya-Rose, 'Its the
Ramshackle gang. What are they doing?'

'The Ramshackles. Can't be!'

'They're stuck in bubbles. Let's get closer.'

Up close I could see Regal, trapped inside this
giant bubble,waving her arms and shouting. But I
couldn't hear a word.

'They can't get out! With any luck this might
work,' said Mya-Rose. She pressed the emerald
against the bubble which instantly burst, soaking
Regal in an foamy liquid.

'Look out. Behind you'!' she yelled as she went
into flying mode.

'It's OK, it's a griffin.'

'No, it's not OK,' said Regal, 'he will rip us to
pieces.'

'Don't think so,' I said, 'she's our friend and
been with us all the way home.'

The griffin flapped her wings and hovered by
our side as Mya- Rose burst the other bubbles. A

soggy Madeleine emerged from her slimy prison. 'I used to like bubbles,' she said, twirling her arms to keep her balance in the air. 'Been stuck in these things for ages. Hey,Willow! You're flying!'

'I know!'

'I'm still not happy about him,' said Regal, keeping a distance from the griffin.

'*He* is a *she* and she won't hurt you. She's coming with us to get her baby back.'

'The one that we have at the house?' said Jax.

'Yeah, the one that you brought home. It's OK, she knows we are friends.'

'Where did you go? asked Coral, flying alongside, 'we were so worried, that's why we came after you, until something put us in these bubbles. I thought we would never get out.'

'It's a long story,' I said.

'Yes, and it can wait till we get back to base,' said Regal, tapping my arm. 'You've got some explaining to do, Willow.'

And so we landed back at Ramshackle House, the wonderful Griffin touching down in the meadow at the back. Her eagle head darting from side to side, She drew in her wings and waited. Running into the kitchen I was scared that the baby griffin might have disappeared, but he was still there in his basket, sharing the space with Suki, who still didn't look very impressed. I picked him up and stroked his head. He gently pecked at my hand and squeaked softly. 'OK, sorry to have let you go but guess what? Your Mummy's waiting for you outside'. Everyone else followed me out into the meadow.

'Just put him down on the ground, he'll find his own way, ' said Regal, not wanting me to get too close.

'No way, I started this and I want to be the one to give him back.' I've never seen an eagle smile and certainly not a griffin. They always look so ferocious, but today I am certain this one did. If you count a griffin as an eagle. I walked towards the griffin and held up the baby. The griffin shrieked so loudly the meadow vibrated. But it was a shriek of joy. She gently picked up the baby, licked his head and then tucked him in a pouch at her side.

You are special girl Willow, you get back my baby

I put my arms round her neck and heard the others gasp. Birdgirl did the same.

We be friends

'We will always be your friend,' I said

'Yes, we will be friends, you saved us. And we will come and see you,' said Mya-Rose.

The griffin tipped her head towards us. Then turned her body round and, with a piercing cry, unfurled her wings and hurtled

into the sky. We stood watching as the griffin headed westwards until she became a tiny dot before she disappeared into the clouds.

'Wow! That was awesome!' said Joel, 'those wings were massive!"

'That was the bravest thing I've ever seen!' said Coral.

'Lets go back inside and you and Birdgirl can tell us all about your adventures,' said Regal.

I led the way back to Ramshackle House, the others following.

'Willow?'

'What?'

'Willow, you can SEE!' said Coral.

The others stopped.

I took a deep breath and blew out my cheeks.

'Mmm, a little bit, yes, I can.'

'Oh, Wow!' Coral jumped in the air and hugged me. 'I don't believe it.'

I think it took the rest of the day for Mya-Rose and me to tell the others about our adventures out there in the Land of the Wicked Way. I don't think I've talked so much in all my life. Coral and Joel made iced buns and we sat around the table drinking strawberry lemonade as we celebrated. Then Regal stood up and announced that she had something very important to say. She looked very serious.

'Today we are fortunate that we can all meet together. .We are safe and we are back. But it could have been a very different ending. What you did, Willow, when you stepped into the hub without permission, was to put us all in grave danger. It could have been the end of of the Ramshackles forever.'

The room fell silent. My smile disappeared. 'I'm really, really sorry, I didn't realise and then it was too late.'

'You will never go into that hub again Willow-!'

'No, I won't, I promise, but please let me stay. I'll make cakes everyday and I'll never give you any more trouble, please don't make me leave-'

'Willow. Stand up and let me finish,' said Regal. 'I was about to say you will never go into the hub again as an unknown, untrained imposter. Because today we have a new Ramshackle Warrior. And it's you, Willow.'

I couldn't say anything. The others screamed and danced around me. 'And I think you've done enough training already!' She moved towards me. 'So I hereby officially announce that Willow is our new Ramshackle warrior and I award her the

Ramshackle gold medal, the highest honour for bravery.' She looped the medal over my head.

'Thank you, thank you so much. This means everything to me,' I said, reaching out for Mya-Rose, 'but I couldn't have done it without Mya-Rose. I wouldn't have got back and I wouldn't be able to see again if it wasn't for her. The hub told me to find Birdgirl. Not only did I find Birdgirl but I found my new best friend. I shall never forget you, Mya-Rose.'

'And we haven't forgotten Mya-Rose,' said Regal, awarding her a gold medal too. 'You are both awesome, and thanks to you, Orcusa has been banished and the birds will once again sing sweetly everyday.'

I was so desperate for Mya-Rose to stay forever but I knew that couldn't happen.

'I have to go back to my homeland, that's where I belong. But you can come and find me again. I'll be there, waiting for our next adventure.'

Choking back my tears, I held the precious emerald stone in my hand one last time as I said goodbye to Mya-Rose, the most amazing girl I have ever met in my life.

I watched her fly away.

The End

Finding Birdgirl

I first saw Mya-Rose Craig, also known as Birdgirl, being interviewed on the BBC One Show alongside Chris Packham about two years ago. I was amazed to hear that Mya-Rose is the youngest person ever to see half the world's bird population. She has also been featured on BBC Springwatch and Countryfile. When I decided to write a fantasy adventure for young children about the environment, I wanted to include Mya-Rose as her fictional self. I think it's incredible how many similarities there are between fact and fiction. Like her character in the book, Mya-Rose loves adventure. She is determined, heroic and brave. She is also passionate about her beliefs and fights against injustice and inequality for the causes she believes in. I called this book *Saving Birdgirl* because 'Save' is a word that Mya-Rose uses many times in her talks and her writing. Saving not just birds but saving all wildlife, saving our environment, saving our world.

Florence

My four year old granddaughter, Florence, loves nature, especially running through the flower meadows and corn fields The world is changing and we must do everything to ensure the children of today have a future.

For me, the most lasting image of Mya-Rose is of her standing on an ice floe on her own in the Arctic ocean, highlighting the devastating effects climate change is having on this region. It was the world's most northerly climate protest ever. Mya-Rose said about the Arctic at the time. 'this is so beautiful and could be all gone by the time I reach thirty.'

Mya-Rose is now officially Dr Mya-Rose Craig, having received an honoury doctorate in 2019 from Bristol University. I feel honoured and very privileged to write a book about this extraordinary young lady. She has achieved many great things in her life. I believe her work is just beginning. I think that in a hundred years time, people will still know the name of Mya-Rose, Birdgirl.

Now meet Birdgirl!

My name is Mya-Rose Craig, I also go by the name Birdgirl. I am an 18 year old British Bangladeshi birder, Conservationist and environmentalist. I have been birding all my life. I obtained my BTO ringing licence when I turned 16 and at 17 became the youngest person to see half the birds of the world.

I am committed to saving nature, campaigning to stop biodiversity loss and climate breakdown, whilst respecting indigenous people and highlighting Global Climate Justice as it intersects with Climate Change Action. I focus my attention on change from governmental and huge global corporations.

My first school report (age 4) said 'Mya-Rose is a spirited and affectionate member of the class! She has so much to give. It is a pleasure to share her thoughts, ideas and experiences and she does so readily. Mya-Rose's strong sense of her own identity is evident, which is lovely to see and she has a lovely sense of humour. In the playground,

Mya-Rose has also recently enjoyed setting up an 'ant community." I think this still just about sums me up!

I write a blog, Birdgirl, and give talks. I spoke on a shared stage with Greta Thunberg in Bristol at a youth strike for climate in March in 2019. I have also written articles for magazines and newspapers including The Times, The Daily Express and The Guardian. I have also appeared on TV and radio. I was a Minister in Chris Packham's People's Manifesto for Wildlife and spoke at his People's Walk for Wildlife. I have also presented a German-French documentary about the decline of grassland and farmland bird species. In 2014 I was listed with George Ezra as one of Bristol's most influential young people. I was also Bristol European Green Capital Ambassador in 2015. I was privileged to meet Sir David Attenborough. He is a legend and has achieved so much, getting ordinary people to be interested in nature, birds and animals. I also loved meeting Chris Packham,

Bill Oddie, Steve Backshall, Miranda Krestovnikoff, Michaela Strachan and Mike Dilger. It was particularly great to meet Bill Oddie as he made birding interesting and fun.

I set up an Extinction Rebellion group, involved with Youth Strikes in 2019. I am involved with Youth for our Planet working to stop species loss and have attended lots of meetings at Downing Street and Parliament. In February 2020, I became the youngest person to be awarded an honorary Doctorate of Science for my five years campaigning with my organisation Black2Nature, which is leading the fight for equal access to the natural environment for Visible Minority Ethnic people. I also organise teenage and children's nature camps and high profile conferences, focusing on race, equality and campaigning to make the sector ethnically diverse. In September 2020, I visited the Arctic with Greenpeace, highlighting the second lowest sea ice minimum and doing the most northerly youth strike ever.

Mya-Rose's climate protest in the Arctic

I also want to combine my obsession for nature and wildlife with my love of adventure. I would like to be a nature and factual television presenter, going on expeditions to remote places and looking for rare species, like Steve Backshall. My biggest passion is world birding which I am very privileged to have had the chance to do. I love birding in my garden and at my local patch, Chew Valley Lake. Twitching (searching out rare birds) is my guilty addiction which I just can't seem to give up and I still get a thrill every time I see a new bird.

Mya-Rose

Follow Mya-Rose on <u>www.birdgirluk.com</u>
twitter @Birdgirl.Uk , <u>Instagram@birdgirluk</u>
and Facebook.

Photographer:Helena Craig

Kelvin is an award-winning playwright and occasional broadcaster. He has his own Radio show on Radio Addenbrooke's in Cambridge. He was previously Head of Year for nineteen years at Sawston Village College, a comprehensive school in Cambridgeshire. He has run drama groups for both secondary and primary schools and spent two years as Film and TV teacher at the Pauline Quirke Academy of Performing Arts. He has also written and directed community films for young people, including The Emma Rolph story for Cambridge Television.

Kelvin enjoys music and wildlife. He saw the Beatles perform live on stage in 1963. In recent times bird watching and walking in the countryside have become regular features during lockdown.

Kelvin is married with three grown up children and six grandchildren. He lives with his wife, Susan, and keeps a pet Royal python called Monty, who is twenty two years old, named after the Aztec Emperor Montezuma. He lives in

Soham, on the outskirts of the Fens in Cambridgeshire.

Acknowledgements

Thank you to **Helena Craig** for photograph, information and support.

Rachel Levitt and the members of the Burwell book Club for introducing me to some wonderful books that otherwise I would never have read. BBC Springwatch team. So inspiring and passionate in all they do. Thank you Chris, Iolo, Michaela, Gillian and Megan,

Greenpeace for giving permission to use the photo of Mya-Rose in the Arctic. Photographer: **Daniella Zalcman**

Front Cover: **Dreamstime.** Photographer: **Alexandra Barbu**

My three daughters-in law Gillian, Gemma, and Faye who have done amazing things over the last difficult year to inspire my grandchildren to read and experience nature.

Shane Reynolds for technical advice

Ava Stephenson-Hyde, may she continue to love books!

Jennifer Killick, a writer of amazing talent and great humour who always offers inspiring and encouraging words of support to others.

To my robin, sadly no longer with us, who gave me one of the most wonderful experiences of my life: To feed a wild bird in my garden every day by hand.

And finally, thank you to everyone who reads this book.

Kelvin Reynolds

Author photographer: Becca Baker